MY EX'S GRUMP BROTHER

NATALIE BELLE

1

AMELIA

I blinked. His lips were moving, but I couldn't make out whatever was coming out of his lips. Surely, I had heard him wrong. There was no way this man was saying what I thought he was saying to me.

"Lia, are you listening to me?" Jacob's hazel eyes looked at me with mild concern. "Did you hear what I said, Lia?"

"I mean, I heard you, but..." my voice trailed off, looking at the ugly picture on the side of his living room. I had always hated that painting, but he said it was an abstract masterpiece.

"Amelia." He called my name again. "Come on. I'm trying to be serious here, and you keep zoning out like what I'm saying isn't important."

I scoffed.

"Do you find this funny?" His bushy eyebrows pulled over his hazel eyes. To think those were the eyes I had once thought were the most beautiful thing I had ever seen. And now, as he looked at me, I couldn't feel that life and devotion that had been there before. I couldn't feel the warmth radiating from them.

"No," I said with a straight face. "I find none of this funny. I came here thinking I would have pancakes with my boyfriend while we binge-watched Stranger Things, but instead, I get you breaking up with me. I don't find any of this funny, Jacob."

He winced.

I hardly ever called him Jacob. I always thought it was too formal. To me, he had always been Jake or Jay. But now, sitting across from him, I couldn't bring myself to call either of those names.

"Look, Lia. I don't—"

"Don't you dare say you don't want to hurt me when you are breaking my heart right now?" I ran a hand through my brown hair. My eyes looked everywhere that wasn't him because I couldn't look into those eyes right now.

"Amelia…" his voice trailed off.

"Why?" I spoke against the lump that had formed in my throat. "Why are you doing this to us? To me?"

It felt like a rock had lodged its way into my chest. With every beat my heart tried to make- it felt like it broke a little more.

The air around me grew thicker, and it felt like I couldn't get enough into my lungs. I pressed my hand over my chest, willing my heart to keep beating even though it was on the verge of shattering.

"I just…" he ran a hand over his face, his eyes looking thoroughly and utterly destroyed.

It was almost comical how he was the one detonating the bomb, yet he looked to be in more pain than I was.

How was that possible?

This was my moment to be destroyed and broken, yet here he was, trying to steal my thunder from me. This was so typical of Jacob.

"You don't get to cry, Jacob. You don't get to be sad." I

stood up from the loveseat we had been on. I stared down at the man I had loved for six years with nothing but ice and hurt in my heart. "You are breaking up with me, and you can't even tell me the bloody reason why. I dedicated six years of my life to you, to this relationship. I gave you my entire heart and soul, and this is what you do to me? We just celebrated our anniversary three days ago when you told me that I was the love of your life. How did that all change in the span of 72 hours?"

By the time I was done ranting, my chest was heaving up and down, and the rage in my blood was spreading like wildfire. The momentary breaking of my heart had been halted, and the anger was taking over.

"What changed, Jacob?" I glared down at him. I wished that looks could kill because I would have this idiot six feet under.

Okay, no. I wouldn't wish him dead but wanted him to hurt now.

"What changed?" I asked again when he didn't answer me the first time. "You can't be this cruel to toy with me. What changed, Jacob? You owe me that much at the very least."

He shrugged, not even bothering to use his words.

Without thinking, I grabbed the closest thing to me, which happened to be his phone, and threw it at the wall.

"Amelia!" He roared. "What the hell is wrong with you? That's my phone."

"Answer me, dammit! When did this all change?"

He looked at me like I had completely lost it, and maybe I had. But he was breaking my heart right now, and I didn't care how I looked. I just wanted to know. I needed to know.

What the hell had I done wrong?

"Tell me!"

"Six months ago," he seethed. "Is that what you want to

hear? Me telling you any of this will do you no good, Amelia. I'm trying to spare you."

"Spare me?" Was he joking right now? "How is any of this sparing me? You are breaking up with me and telling me you wanted to break up with me six months ago. So, all this time, you led me on for what? Why not just spare me, then? Why now when we were picking out houses together two weeks ago?"

I stepped toward him and pushed his chest hard. All this time I had wasted. All these memories and moments we had shared.

"Why not spare me back then?" I pushed him hard. "Why?"

"Amelia, please." He wanted me to stop, but I was not backing down.

"Why?"

"I wanted to see if I could fall in love with you again." He blurted out in haste.

I stilled. "What?"

"Damn," he cursed under his breath. "I don't want to hurt you any more than I already have, Lia. You are one of my best friends, and I care so much about you. But I just...I don't...."

He didn't love me.

All those years together. All those hopes and dreams we had. What had they all been for?

"You..." my voice trailed off. "You don't love me anymore. That's what you were going to say, right? You would tell me that you don't love me anymore."

"It's not that I don't love you, Lia. It just—"

"Don't call me that," I spat, "you don't get to call me Lia anymore. Only my close people call me that, and you are not one of them."

He looked hurt at my words, but I didn't give a damn.

He was breaking my heart with his words. Why would he do this to me? To us.

"Six years," I choked out. The tears pooled in my eyes, squeezing with every beat I took. "Six years of my life I spent with you. You were the first boy I kissed. The only man who has touched my body. The only man who ever owned my heart."

He looked away.

"You were meant to be my everything, Jacob. You called me your...your...." I couldn't even get the word out.

I tried to blink away the tears, but more would come in their stead each time I tried.

"You were—I mean, you are my ocean, Amelia. But I can't be with you like we are right now. I don't know what I want out of life anymore. I thought being here in Braven Bay and loving you would be enough, but it's just not. My heart needs more. We aren't enough."

Translation, I wasn't enough to make him happy.

"You are still my—"

"Don't you dare." I held my hand up, taking a tentative step back. "Don't you dare be that cruel to me."

If he called me his best friend, it would be like a slap to the face. Best friends were meant to protect each other. They were meant to love each other through all the bad and the good. They were not meant to cause each other harm intentionally; that was what he was doing to me.

He was taking a dagger and lodging it right in my chest. But he wasn't just stopping there. He was twisting it with every reason he gave why he could not be with me.

I shook my head in pure disbelief. "I...I need to go."

I grabbed my overnight bag from his coffee table and left his house, forgetting my shoes. But I didn't dare to turn back. I was never going to turn back.

With my back turned to him and my sights on my car

ahead, I allowed the tears to flow. I allowed myself to break free without anyone else's eyes on me.

I slammed the door to my Volvo shut and roared the engine to life. The tears continued to fall silently down my face, and I allowed myself to shatter in the silence.

All those hopes and dreams came crashing down in seconds —the life I had built in my head. The palaces of his words and promises had painted what I thought nothing but honesty. None of it was real. It had never been confirmed, and I had been a fool to believe that happy endings came for people like me.

Three weeks later…

"You look like shit, babe," Selena, or Lena, as I called her as well, my best friend, said.

She wasn't looking at me directly, however. She was more focused on getting her winged eyeliner right in the mirror.

"I am going through heartbreak. Sue me," I said with a mouth full of Hot Cheetos. I didn't even love Hot Cheetos, but these were the last things in my kitchen. I hadn't left the house in three weeks. Was I hiding from the judgmental society of Braven Bay? Yes, I was not ashamed to say that.

Braven Bay was such a tight-knit community. Everyone knew everyone. We were all in each other's business, meaning everyone likely had already heard about my breakup with Jake.

In high school, we were voted the couple likely to get married and settle in Braven Bay. Well, that aged well.

"Are you listening to me?" Selena peered at me with her full-done face. The blue eye shadow brought out the green in her eyes.

"Where are you going?"

"A date," she smiled. "I haven't gotten laid in a while, and I think it's time the streets of Chicago remember who I am." She shot me a wicked smirk and a wink before she disappeared out of view of the screen.

I had always been so jealous of her. She left Braven Bay after high school, moved to Chicago, and never looked back. Selena was the kind of person who followed the wind in any given direction it blew. She was carefree and lived without caution.

Looking at her, you would never guess she was a paralegal. She lived life like she was dying the next day.

"Who's the guy?" I finally asked, digging into my bag of Cheetos and finding it empty.

Shoot.

"This Italian restaurant owner is named Davide. You should see his arms," she came back into view of the screen with her boobs out and the bathroom towel discarded. "I swear that man is what you would call the Italian stallion."

I rolled my eyes. "Nice to know one of us is getting laid tonight. I wish I had your life. Living it up in a big city without the prying eyeballs of Mama Gertrude and Sydney. Just being you."

"Then why don't you move out to Chicago and come live that life? It'll be 'Lena and Lia take Chicago'"

I laughed, thinking she was making a joke, but my laughter quickly died when I saw that she was serious. "You're serious?"

She stepped into the red showstopper dress before giving me her full attention. "Why not? You've been stuck in Braven Bay all your life, Amelia. Don't you ever wonder what is out there for you? Your entire life has been planned around Jacob, and now that he is out of the picture, you can finally make your life about you. Don't you want to know what the world offers you?"

"I…" venturing beyond Braven Bay had never been a thought for me.

"Don't you want to live for yourself finally? What is left for you in Braven Bay?"

She was right. What was left for me in Braven Bay?

Old memories. And a town full of gossip. People who would only look at me with pity. My mother died when I was six, and my father passed away two years ago. The only person who had kept me here was Jake, and now that he was gone, what was stopping me from just packing up and leaving?

Nothing. Nothing at all.

2

AMELIA

I stared out the window at the city before me. Large concrete buildings stood before me. I could hear the distant sound of sirens in the background.

Chicago was loud and busy, and everyone was on their track.

I loved it.

I had been so used to Braven Bay's slow and quiet life that this was a total change of pace, but I liked it.

"What did you pack in here," Selena placed one of my many boxes on the kitchen counter.

I turned back to smile at my best friend. "My entire life."

Packing up and leaving Braven was a rash and quick decision, but I had no real regrets. I was happy. I was glad to be away from that place but, most importantly, excited to put distance between me and all things Jacob Cane.

I walked over to the white counter and leaned against the excellent granite. "So what do you think?"

"It's nice." She looked around my studio apartment. "It's a good start, all things considered."

The studio had been a stroke of luck. I found it after two

Zillow searches, and it was all within my price range. It had light wood floors and large windows that showed off the Chicago skyline. The kitchen was fitted, and I even had my washer and dryer. I was a happy woman.

"I must give it some Amelia 'pazazz,' but I love it. And it's all mine." My heart felt so content.

I had lived in my childhood home from the moment I was born until the very last day I left Braven. When Dad got sick, I knew I couldn't leave him alone.

It looked like the house you pictured when you thought of that 'American dream.' Consisting of a small yard, a white picket fence, a wraparound wooden porch, an American flag hanging next to the front door, and a homey atmosphere that draws you in. I loved it for a time. It was where I pictured raising my children with—

"No," Selena shook my shoulders. "Stop thinking about that idiot."

"I wasn't." I was.

"Yes, you were. I saw it on your face. You had that mopey dopey look in your eyes." She gave me this look that meant she could see right through my bullshit. "He's in your past, babes. Leave him behind there. This is your future, okay?" She gestured to the studio.

I let out a low sigh. "You're right. I need to focus on the here and the now."

"Atta girl. Now get the rest of your boxes. I am not lugging those things out of the U-haul anymore. I have delicate hands, you know."

I rolled my eyes at her and left the apartment.

I took my phone from my pocket and started scrolling through my Instagram. I had been avoiding social media for the sole purpose of not seeing anything about Jake.

I had unfollowed him but still followed many of our mutual friends back home. Well, they were more his friends than mine. I had just adopted them as my friends seeing as we were with them whenever we went out together as a couple.

Now that I had stepped away from that bubble I had been in, I could see how much of my life had been absorbed by Jacob. He had never asked me to mold our lives together like that, but I had been the one to do it.

I wanted us to be one. I wanted us to intertwine the way we had been.

I scrolled through my feed, and sure enough, I saw a picture of him with his friends on Banto Lake back in Braven. They were all smiling at the camera, holding beers.

They looked like they were having a grand old time. You wouldn't even believe this was the same man who had said he would cease breathing if we weren't together.

Well, why weren't you suffocating, Jacob?

This wasn't healthy. Checking up on him like this through his friends' socials was a bad idea. If I wanted to move on, I needed actually to move on.

I went into my following, unfollowed all our mutual friends, and placed my phone back in my pocket. The elevator doors dinged, and I stepped into the four-walled space.

Each one of the walls was made up of mirrors so that I could see myself from every angle.

For the first time in over a month, I could see glimpses of the girl I used to be—the one that was carefree, happy, and in love with life. For the first time, my hazel eyes shone. They didn't seem so dulled out and tired.

I was still hurt and heartbroken, but I knew I would heal. I would survive Jacob, just like how I had endured the loss of my parents. That's what I did. I survived. But now, after licking my wounds, I wanted to thrive.

"Welcome back, Lia." I smiled at my reflection just as the

elevator doors dinged open. I stepped out of the elevator with an extra kick in my step. But unfortunately for me, I didn't see the wet floor sign on the tiled floors before I slipped and crashed into someone.

I heard a loud grunt, and we both fell to the ground, the man underneath me taking the brunt of the fall.

My cheeks flamed at my embarrassment as I scrambled to my feet. "I am so sorry I didn't—"

My words caught in my throat as I watched the rather muscular, tall man get up. But that was not what caused me to pause.

Remember how I said I had left all things Jacob back in Braven? I was wrong because I was staring into a pair of green eyes I had not seen in almost a decade.

"Nate?" His name sounded so foreign on my lips.

The green eyes glared down at me. "You have the wrong person."

He stepped to the side, but I blocked his path.

"No, no. I am sure you are Nathaniel Arthur Cane, brother to Jacob Ezekiel Cane." It was like I was looking at a ghost. "It's been a while since I last saw you, but you are Nate."

His eyes narrowed, and his nostrils flared a little.

"There." I pointed at his nose. "You and Jacob do the same nose thing when you get mad. You're his brother!" They looked nothing alike. Their only similarity was that they had the same brown locks they inherited from their mother. This man was Nathaniel Cane. He had to be.

You don't forget green eyes like his easily.

"Congratulations. Do you want a prize?" I was taken aback by the iciness in his voice. "Move."

"You don't have to be rude."

"You ran into me and made me fall. You could have taken my back out," He grunted.

I rolled my eyes.

"Calm down. No need to be dramatic. At most, you have a bruised tailbone."

He huffed in frustration.

He stared at me like he wanted to shoot me down where I stood, and I didn't know why. I hardly knew the guy. In all the time I had dated Jake, I had met him ten times. And each time, it was in passing. I always felt he didn't like me, but now, standing before him, I was taken aback by how much.

"Have I offended you in some way?"

"No."

"Then why are you looking at me like you want to kill me."

"Maybe because you barreled me down like a fucking bulldozer."

"Bulldozer? I slipped."

"There was a sign warning about a wet floor," he said with a deadpan face.

"I…"

"Exactly. Now get out of my way. I've had a long day."

Then it struck me. "You live in this building?"

He just stared at me.

Oh great. I had run away from one Cane only to find myself in the presence of another.

This was the last thing that I needed right now.

"Okay." I needed to try a different approach. "I don't know how much your brother has told you, but I—"

"I don't care." He said, taking a step towards me. He leered down at me with this angry-looking face. "I don't care what is happening between you and Jacob. Quite frankly, I could give a shit about it. Now, if you would be so kind as to get out of my way so I can get to my apartment. You stay out of my way, and I will stay out of yours. Sound good?"

Before I could answer, he brushed past me and walked

into the awaiting elevator. I turned just in time to watch the doors close, and our eyes made contact.

A cold shiver ran down my spine at how he looked at me. There was so much hatred in his gaze that I didn't even understand what I had done to him. I barely knew the guy. Yet, it felt like we had unfinished business for some reason.

I shook off the odd feeling and made my way out of the building to go and get the last of my belongings.

Why could I not escape these damn Cane men? They were like a nasty rash. No matter what ointment you used, they always came back.

3

NATHANIEL

I pushed my legs harder, the Chicago air cooling my body as we ran down the block. The morning sun still hid behind the large buildings.

I needed this. A run always helped to calm me. After the little surprise I had received yesterday, I needed to clear my head.

Why the hell was she here? In my city of all places.

I had left Braven Bay behind me many years ago, but somehow it always seemed to find a way to pull me back into its cold icy grip. I had left that place for many reasons, her being one of them.

I pushed my legs even harder, picking up my pace. I didn't bother to look behind me to see if Xander was still behind me.

Her face filtered into my mind, and all that rage flooded my mind again. Those big hazel eyes haunted me. They had been in the back of my mind for over a decade. She had plagued me and been only a mere ghost. Until I came face to face with them again when my brother brought her over for

Thanksgiving dinner. He had wanted to introduce us to his new girlfriend, and I had lost my shit completely.

It was her.

I pushed my legs harder and faster until I came to a halt just outside 'The Bean House.'

"Are…what the hell?" Xander came to a stop beside me. He doubled over, trying to catch his breath. "This was meant to be an easy morning. What the hell, man?"

"You looked like you needed an extra push today."

He snapped his neck up at me and gave me his best glare. "I said take it easy. You looked like you were running like demons were hot on your tail."

They were to some extent, but I was not ready to divulge that information. At least not yet.

"I feel like my spleen is about to implode on itself." He grabbed me. "Hell. Death by morning jog is not how I imagined I would go out. I always thought it would be a blonde with perky tits and a big ass."

I brushed his hand off of mine. "You are disgusting. You would want to die while having sex?"

"Is there any other way to go?" The bastard smirked. "Come on. You owe me a coffee and possibly a new lung."

"I told you to lay off the beers last night."

"It was a Friday night. What did you want me to drink? Green juice? That's for the mornings after yoga."

I stared at my best friend like he had lost his marbles. Had he just said what I thought he had said? "Since when do you do yoga?"

A mischievous glint took over his brown eyes. "Since Monica from the third floor showed me yoga is good for flexibility. Oh man, she does this thing with her leg that I—"

"No," I said, walking into the little coffee shop, leaving him to speak to himself. There was no way I would sit around and listen to him talk about sex.

Xander followed in after me. We were immediately hit with the smell of coffee grounds and hot muffins.

"Get my usual for me, please. I need to go and relieve myself." Xander walked off toward the bathroom. But not before shamelessly ogling the waitress whom I was sure he had a thing with not too long ago.

From how this man behaved, you would not think he ran into burning buildings for a living. He acted more like a frat boy than an actual firefighter.

I walked over to the front counter to place my order. But as I approached, I heard the one voice I didn't want to hear.

"With some cold foam on the top, please." Why did she have to sound so damn chipper in the morning? It was six in the morning. "No, you can keep the change. Have a great day."

Amelia turned to leave the register but came face to face with me again.

Why did I always seem to have the misfortune of bumping into her?

"Oh, Nate."

I ground my teeth. "Don't call me that."

No one except for my family and close friends called me Nate. To others, I was Cane or Nathaniel. And I rarely answered Nathaniel either way.

"Well, aren't you just a ray of sunshine so early in the morning." The sarcasm oozed into her tone.

I huffed and went to move past her. I heard her mutter something under her breath, but I didn't bother turning back to question her. The less interaction with her I had, the better for me.

I placed my order and then went to wait for our coffees, but I stopped short when I noticed Xander with none other than the woman I wanted to stay as far away from as possible.

I ground my teeth together with the annoyance building in my body.

As I neared them, I watched Xander's eyes twinkle with glee. He wanted her, which only added to my annoyance.

"Oh, really, and how would you figure that?" Amelia laughed.

Her laugh did something to my insides. I couldn't quite explain the feeling, but it was intrusive and caught me off guard.

Xander proceeded to say something else, making her laugh.

What the hell was so funny?

I cleared my throat and settled into the seat next to Xander. I didn't pay her attention. I pretended she didn't even exist in my eyes.

Childish? Maybe. But who the hell cared? She had walked into my city without warning. She was the one in the wrong here.

"Nate, let me introduce you to the lovely—"

"I know who she is," I interrupted him, ignoring her. "Our orders should be ready."

In my peripheral, I could see the frown come over her face.

"How do you two know each other?" He looked between us. "Did you two used to bump nasties?"

"Not in this lifetime or the next." It was Amelia who answered quickly.

I cocked an eyebrow, "And why is that?"

"You just aren't my cup of tea, to put it in nice terms. And besides, I think having sex with you would be like having sex with a cardboard box. You have zero expression or passion. I can't do that."

My frown deepened.

"But me, on the other hand," Xander drawled. "I might as well be Italian. I am the perfect lover, if you didn't know."

Amelia giggled, which annoyed me.

"What would my brother think if he saw you shamelessly flirting with other men? Never pegged you as a cheater."

Her shoulders tensed, and the smile was wiped clean off her face. A sadness took over her eyes, and for a split second, she looked slightly hurt by my words before she fixed her features.

"If you must know, Jacob and I broke up almost a month ago. I highly doubt he will care if I'm flirting with anyone."

This was news to me. Granted, I didn't speak to my brother often, except for the occasional monthly check-ins. But I could have sworn he had once called this girl his entire world.

His devotion to her was what angered me the most. After all, she had done to our family. But then again, he didn't know about Amelia and mine's connection from 16 years earlier; he wasn't there.

"Wait a minute; you were with baby Cane?" Xander let out a low laugh. "How did that asshole land you? No offense to the guy, but you are a straight ten. I mean, you are a total knockout."

"Xander," I didn't like how he kept talking to her like they were chums—the more distance between her and me, the better. I didn't need to be befriending the woman responsible for my family's pain.

Amelia blushed. "I don't know about all that, but thank you, I guess."

Amelia's name was called in the background for her order pick-up.

"That's me," she said, smiling at Xander. "It was nice meeting you, Xander. Hopefully, I will see you around and next time with a more agreeable company."

The slight dig my way was cute and unnecessary. She didn't need to sit with us.

Technically, I had come to sit with them. But Xander was my friend. God, I sounded like a jealous teen girl.

"I will see you around." I noticed him handing her a phone—her phone. "I have your number, and I took the liberty of putting in my number for you. Maybe we can grab coffee sometime."

I ground my teeth together, but I didn't say anything.

Amelia's blush deepened, and she left us by ourselves.

When she was out of earshot, I slapped my best friend upside down.

"Ow, what was that for?" He pouted like a child. "First my lungs and now my skull? What the hell?"

"Stay away from her," I said

"Why?"

"Because I said so."

"That's not reason enough, I'm afraid. Is it because she is your brother's ex?"

That should have been the main reason, but it wasn't. It was something much deeper than that. Something that I had never told a single soul.

"Yeah, it would be too messy. She and Jacob have a long history."

And so did me and her.

4

AMELIA

I scrolled through my emails and smiled at all the responses I had gotten. Working as a freelance photographer, you never truly knew how the business would go. But moving here to Chicago has already proved more profitable for my business.

I loved taking pictures of newborns and pregnant women. There was something so beautiful about these little lives that were being formed.

It was always a dream of mine to have my little mini-me. To grow a life in my belly with someone I love. I was halfway there with that dream until Jake ended it all.

I quickly shook my head and removed all thoughts of my treacherous ex. I was starting a new life and was sure I would find a new love. Maybe not now, but in the future, I was sure. I was worthy of being loved by a man wholly and fully.

I had just finished my schedule for the month when I heard a knock at the door. I got up from my bed and made my way to it. When I opened the door, I was met with forest-green eyes.

"Nate?"

His passive face turned into a frown when I said his name.

"Oh, sorry, Nathaniel." I corrected myself, realizing I used a name only reserved for a special few. "What are you doing here?"

"My shower isn't working," he said like I should understand why he was at my door at seven in the morning.

"Okay, sorry?"

"I need to use yours."

His request threw me a little. Last I checked, the man wanted nothing to do with me, and now he was knocking at my door asking for favors.

"Are you asking or demanding?"

"Does it matter?" He shrugged.

"Yes, it does. You can't just come to someone's door demanding things, especially when you don't like the other person in question."

He stared at me blankly.

"Can't you ask someone else? Last I checked, you didn't want to be within a fifty feet radius of me."

"Trust me, if I could help it, I would not be here right now. I came here as a last resort."

"You aren't helping your case as to why I should even help you."

He let out an exasperated sigh. "I have work in the next hour and need a shower."

"Say, please."

He cocked an eyebrow. "Seriously?"

"It would be the polite thing to do. Don't you think?" I crossed my arms over my chest.

"May I please use your shower, Amelia?"

My face split into a megawatt smile. "Since you asked so nicely, you can."

I stepped aside and allowed him to come into the small

studio apartment. Nathan stepped inside, his large frame taking up significant space. I closed the door behind me and stared at him for a moment.

It astounded me how he and Jacob could be related. They were opposites in every single way. Nathan was built like a freaking tank, whereas Jacob had this nerdier skinny vibe going for him. Where Jacob still had that boyish charm, Nathaniel was a full-blown man. The stubble on his jaw only added to that rugged look.

Heat poured into my veins, and I quickly reminded myself that this was my unofficial nemesis. He was not my friend, and there was no way I could feel any kind of...feelings for him.

"The bathroom is right over there." I pointed to the only door in my studio. "It's small, so may have to umm...squeeze."

He gave me something between a hum and a grunt.

He walked into the bathroom and locked the door behind him. I stood in my place until I heard the turning on of the water.

I walked back to the kitchen island and finished what I had been doing before I decided to go and start on my breakfast.

I tried my best not to think about the naked man in my bathroom, but it was hard.

My brain turned to absolute mush whenever I was near him. He moved something in me. I didn't know precisely what he moved, but I knew it was terrible.

I poured my yogurt over my granola and scrolled through my phone. I had done my best to stay off social media—it was part of my healing journey.

Okay, not really. I was trying not to self-combust in fear of somehow seeing him on my Instagram feed.

As I scrolled through my feed, I caved and looked up his profile. I wanted to see it for curiosity purposes.

I leaned my elbows against the granite tabletop.

There he was, Jacob_Cane145.

My heart thundered in my chest as I scrolled down his profile. All traces of me had been erased. The trip that we took to Bali only eight months ago. All of Valentine's posts he had made of me. Even in his highlights titled 'home🖤' the man had removed me from there too.

My heart squeezed a little.

I had removed him from my social media, but his doing it felt so permanent because Jacob didn't remove anything from his social media. He always said it was like his digital diary. He wanted people to see his life story.

I had always thought it was a dumb notion, but now it felt like he had erased me from his diary. I was no longer a part of his life, and I had been axed from him.

Six years of loving each other. All the tears and laughs. All the memories and unfulfilled plans.

We were going to take a trip to Paris next year. I had even mapped out an entire itinerary. For so long, I had envisioned him as a permanent fixture in my life that the idea of not having him here tore at something in my heart.

It was no longer a plan for two but a project for one.

Why had I not been enough? Why could he not have just stayed?

The sting built behind my eyes, and I had to blink away the unshed tears. He didn't deserve my tears; no man deserved them.

For too long, I had allowed myself to compromise my hopes and dreams for someone else. I had allowed myself to take a back seat to accommodate others and make them feel seen and wanted. All the while, I neglected the most important person—me.

I was so deep in thought that I did not notice the significant presence behind me until I whirled around, wanting to check on my breakfast, and rammed into his very naked chest.

"Jesus," I pressed a hand over my heart and peered at him. "Announce yourself next time. You can't just sneak up on me."

"I called your name three times, but you didn't answer me." He stared into my eyes with those haunting eyes of his. "Are you hard of hearing?"

"What?" I choked on my saliva. "Is that any way to thank someone who let you use their water to clean off your BO?"

He cocked an eyebrow. "BO?"

"Yes, as in Body Odor. You know, smelly pits. The stuff that comes out when you sweat a lot and don't use deodorant."

"I didn't have BO."

"Fun fact, most people can't smell their own BO."

He blinked at me for a moment. He looked both confused and annoyed.

The tension intensified. Then, suddenly my brain did that mushy thing.

"Would you like some breakfast?" I cleared my throat, trying to look anywhere but his eyes. My gaze drifted lower, and my, oh my.

Then, I took him in entirely in all his half-naked glory. The man was fresh out of the shower and had no shirt on, which meant his very chiseled chest was on full display—all for my sex-deprived eyes to drink in.

That day I ran into him and Xander in the café; he wore a tight-fitting shirt. I knew that he was fit, but nothing like this.

The heavens themselves perfectly chiseled his chest. Some

people were just blessed, and it was completely and utterly unfair.

One thing I did notice was the scar that rang vertically down the side of his torso. My eyes were transfixed on it. It looked like a wound of some sort.

Nathaniel had been in the military for five years and had done tours in some of the harshest places on the face of the earth. It only made sense that he came away with a few battle scars.

"What happened?" I voiced the roaring question in my mind. "Over there."

I pointed to his scar, and he tensed.

His features hardened, and all the friendless, if you could even call it that, left his body.

"None of your business. Thanks for the shower." He turned to leave my apartment without so much as a look back. I couldn't even get a 'you're welcome' out before the door slammed.

What an ass.

I wondered why he was so touchy about his scar. Maybe I had crossed a line and brought up a memory he had long wanted to forget.

Great, now I feel like a jackass.

5

NATHANIEL

We were cleaning off our gear after a house fire, and my mind started wandering back to a certain brunette with toned legs and a smart mouth.

I scrubbed my boots hard, trying to work her out of my mind.

She was not meant to be back here. She was not meant to be in my city and wreaking havoc like this.

She was in trouble, and she didn't even know it. How my little brother had handled her all those years, I don't even know.

"Are you even listening to me, Nate?" Xander's voice brought me out of my thoughts.

"What?"

"I was talking about your new neighbor, Amelia." He wiggled his eyebrows.

"I told you that she's off limits."

He held up his hands, dropping his cleaning equipment. "I'm not saying I don't want to put the girl in my bed and have my way with her. I would love to have her ass up, face down but—ow! That hurt you, asshole."

"Good."

He rubbed his shoulder where I had thrown a brush at him.

"I bruise easily. What will Kesha say when she sees me all purple and blue."

"Kesha?"

His lips split into a sly smirk, and I nearly hit him again.

"Do you ever take a break from women?"

"There are just far too many in this world not to love. Who am I to deny them some good old sloppy toppy?"

"Sloppy toppy?"

"Becca, this college senior, told me it means good, down, and dirty—"

"Finish that sentence, and I will cut your dick off in your sleep." I did not need to know what that word meant. I was too old to learn things like that, and so was he.

I was only 31, but the things I had seen while away had aged me at least ten years or more.

Going into war zones and taking on bullets, shrapnel, and death was not for the faint of heart. I watched children get gunned down in front of my very eyes. I watched women forced to give birth in hospitals that were being bombed.

Seeing things like that charred some parts of your soul, and you never quite recovered from stuff like that.

The crash. The rain. Her screams.

That night played so vividly in my head that you would swear I was living through it again.

"Can we finish up here so we can get lunch?" I steered my thoughts away from that night when the first burn left a mark on me.

"Fine. But I must tell you what happened when I visited

Becca's. The girl took me to a rave." Xander continued to drone on about his date with the spunky 22-year-old.

Usually, I didn't like hearing him speak about his sex life, but I needed to distract my mind from what was taking over my thoughts.

I needed to stop thinking about her. And I needed to stop thinking about that night.

It would do me no good, especially now that she was back in town. Those were demons I would instead let lie.

By the time we got our shit in order, it was lunch. Xander and K climbed into my truck and started towards the little deli shop near the station. The idiot buried his head in his phone, choosing whoever was his next victim.

The man had no rest.

I parked along the sidewalks where 'Papa Panini' was located.

"Dipshit." I grabbed his phone that he couldn't let go of and looked at what he was doing. To my surprise, the little asshole was texting none other than the woman I told to leave alone. "Seriously? I thought I told you that you couldn't talk to her."

He grabbed his phone back. "The girl is a good person, Nate. I don't get why you are such an ass to her. She just moved here and wants to feel more at home."

"And how exactly do you plan on making her feel at home? Balls deep in her?"

He scowled at me. "I promised you I wouldn't go there, and I meant every word. I won't go there. But I am going to be her friend. She needs one right now."

"I'm sure she has friends."

"One. She could use a few more."

"And how do you know how many friends she has?"

"She told me."

I leaned my head back in my chair.

29

"I won't sleep with the girl but will be her friend. Just because you are a class A asshole to her doesn't mean I need to be one too."

He was right. My connection to her should not affect how he perceived her. But I couldn't afford her getting close to me, not when I had worked so hard to quiet those demons in my head.

"Fine."

Xander smiled and opened his door. "Now hurry up. I'm hungry, and we need to return to the station."

I rolled my eyes and got out of the car.

When we got back to the station, my stomach was full, but my mind wondered about a particular hazel-eyed minx who had come back or haunt me.

"I'm going to lie down," I told Xander as we walked into the station. "My head is killing me."

Xander looked at me, a little concerned. "You good?"

I nodded even though I knew the chaos that was swirling in my body right now.

I got to the resting area and closed my eyes, willing for the peace of sleep to somehow come and calm the storm in my mind.

I don't know how long it took to drift off, but soon I was off to sleep, and my mind had taken me back to a time I wished I could forget.

There was a loud ringing in my ear. My whole world had just flipped on its axis, leaving me disoriented and confused. I didn't know which way was up and which way was down.

Slowly I willed my eyes open even though the pressure in my skull wanted me to rest.

Fire. I could feel the heat of fire not too far away from

me. Glass covered my body, and my seat belt clung to it, keeping it in place.

I turned my head, with great effort, to the side and found my mother. Her eyes were facing forward, her head dripping with blood. Her body shook uncontrollably as her hands held onto a rod lodged in her abdomen.

"Mom?" I croaked. My throat felt like I had swallowed a pack of rusted nails. "Mom?"

She turned her neck in my direction, and my heart caught in the middle of my throat.

"Baby…"

My body surged forward as the alarm blared in my ears.

'Engine 68, school fire 3564 Willow Grove Ave,' the alarm blared.

I watched Xander run past me with the rest of my squad, and I hopped out of bed as my instincts kicked in.

I hadn't dreamt of my mother and the accident in over ten years, but the dreams returned. It didn't take a rocket scientist to figure that this had to do with a certain new-to-town woman with a smart-ass mouth.

Amelia Carter would be the death of me.

6

AMELIA

"Come on, you look fine," Selena said as we walked into the entrance of the new bar that had just opened in downtown Chicago.

"I look like a hooker," I muttered, trying to pull up the tight corset showing just a tad bit too much cleavage for my liking. "Did you have to make me wear this? Look at me."

She stopped dead in her tracks and pulled my attention to her. "You are a hot single woman going out on the town. You can't stay cooped up in your apartment like a hermit. You are hot, young, and sexy as fuck. Flaunt those perky boobies before they sag."

"I just…" I looked down at myself. "I'm a little out of my element here."

She placed her hands on my shoulders and squeezed them tightly. "And that is a good thing. You kept in your shell for years, but now it's time to live a little. I know you like coloring inside the lines, but be a little reckless for tonight, okay? Flirt. Make out with a random stranger. Get dunk. I don't care. Just let loose, Lia."

I rolled my shoulder and shook out the trapped tension in my back. "Okay. To a night of bad decisions."

Selena's face split into a shit-eating grin. "That's my girl. Now come on. Let's go con these men into getting us free drinks."

She hooked her arm in mine and walked me to the bar's entrance.

A large neon blue sign read, 'Billy's Well.'

The name could have been better, but the vibes were immaculate as soon as we walked in. The bar was decorated like one of those old Western bars that you saw in the movies. Everything from the furniture to the walls and floors was made of dark wood.

The decorations on the walls comprised various number plates from different states—parts of a motorcycle and some pictures of Chicago sports legends.

The music played through the speakers could only be described as old country bangers.

I didn't miss the way the men in the bar turned to look at us as we walked in.

I wouldn't say we stuck out like sore thumbs, but we didn't exactly blend into the casual appearance of the rest of the bar-goers. While most of them wore jeans and T-shirts, we dressed like we were ready for the club.

Skinny jeans, thigh-high boots, and corset tops rearranged my internal organs.

"This is going to be so fun." She pulled me in, headed straight for the bar area, and placed orders for two gin and tonics.

We had just gotten our drinks when I felt a presence come up beside me. When I turned to my left, I came face to face with a pair of brown eyes.

"Hello there, gorgeous." The guy leaned in toward me, and I could smell the scent of cigarettes on him. Instantly, I was reminded of my pappy, who smoked two packs a day. Pappy also had rotting teeth and picked his ear wax at the dinner table.

"Hey," I smiled at him.

"You look ravishing tonight." His eyes shamelessly went to my cleavage, which was on full display. "Maybe we can get out of here for a bit and head to my place to get to know each other better."

I opened my mouth to speak, but Lena beat me to it.

"Seriously? That is what you are coming with." She scoffed, pulling me closer to her. "I think the kind of woman you are looking for is down a few blocks working the corner."

The guy frowned. "As you can see, we are talking here. So why don't you mind your own business and leave us be." The guy placed his hand over mine, and I kid you not; my whole body shuddered at his touch.

I tried to remove my hand from his, but he held me tightly.

"Asshole, let her go," Selena growled. Her eyes blazed with a fury I had only seen when she was ready to pounce on her victim.

"What are you going to do about it, bitch?"

One moment the guy was standing there, and the next moment, a fist connected with his face, and he was on the ground groaning in pain.

With wide eyes, I turned to look to the side and found Nathaniel leering over the guy with an angry-looking Xander behind him.

"The lady said to let go, dipshit." Nate's voice was laced with venom so potent I could taste its bitterness on my tongue. His fists were balled at his side, and his eyes blazed with the fury of a thousand suns. The anger rolled off of him in waves. It was hard not to feel the heat radiating from him.

Nate picked the guy up and held him from the back of his shirt. "Apologize to the lady."

The guy frowned at me before he tried to have a go at Nate, but that was a dumb idea. Nate ducked his strikes and pressed his face against the wooden bar. He pulled his arm behind him and twisted until the guy screamed in agony.

"Nate, come on," the bartender, who had just served us our drinks, said. "Don't get blood on my bar."

"Got it, Vic." Nate raised the guy so he was looking at me but was still subdued in Nate's hold. "Apologize. Now."

Nate pulled his arm even more.

"Ow! Okay! Okay!" The guy said in agony. "I'm sorry, okay? Happy?"

Nate looked at me for confirmation, to which I just gave a curt nod, completely stunned by what was playing out before me.

"You're lucky she said okay. Otherwise, I was going to break your front teeth and nose. If I ever catch you harassing any other woman in this city, I will fucking break your wrists. Understand?"

Nate pulled on the guy's arm again, and he yelped and nodded.

"Now get out of here."

He let the guy go before he was escorted out by one of the larger-looking guys at the door when we got in. He was likely security.

Nate watched until the guy was out of sight before he turned to me with an unreadable expression.

"You good?" His green eyes searched my face. "Did he hurt you?"

Was he...caring?

The same man who had told me to go and fuck myself had defended me against a misogynistic prick. What a strange turn of events.

"No," I spoke against the thick emotion layer lodged in my throat. "Thank you."

He didn't respond. He just kept staring at me with those brilliant green eyes that took my breath away every time I stared into them.

"Not to interrupt your little eye-blinking session," Selena cleared her throat, causing heat to rise to my cheeks.

"Oh. My. God," Selena said in excitement.

She stepped forward and extended her hand. "You must be the brooding older brother to her annoying ex-boyfriend."

Nathaniel cocked an eyebrow and stared at her hand. "And you are?"

"Selena."

"Like Gomez?" Xander stepped forward, his once glare replaced by a flirtatious smirk.

"No ass," Selena crossed her arms over her chest, causing her boobs to bulge even more. "Like Quintanilla-Peréz. Do I look like a Disney princess to you?"

"You got some fire in you. I like it."

Selena's frown deepened. "Back up walking STD incubator."

"Selena," I hissed, "you can't say that about people."

"Is it not true?" She was looking at Xander. "The man just screams player. I'm sure you have slept through half of the female population in Chicago."

"Just because I enjoy sex casually, that means I have STDs? I will have you know I get tested regularly."

"Good for you." Her tone oozed with sarcasm.

The small group fell silent, and we all just looked at each other, unsure of what to do. Xander and Selena were having some secret stare-off. While Nathanial looked like he wanted to be anywhere but the current place he was standing in.

Then an idea popped into my mind. It was likely a dumb one, but at least it would guarantee to take the edge off.

"Shots, anyone?" I suggested cutting through the awkward silence that had enveloped us.

Xander and Selena both looked at me with matching smiles on their faces. Nathaniel, if possible, scowled even more.

"Hell to the fuck, yes. But I say we make it interesting. We can play a little game." Selena wiggled her eyebrows, looking at all three of us.

"Now you're speaking my language, shortcake." Xander rubbed his hands together.

"Truth or drink."

"Oh no."

"Hell, yes!" Xander clapped his hands and waved to Vic, who stood behind the bar. "Vic, 16 rounds of your strongest tequila, please."

This was a disaster just waiting to happen.

7

AMELIA

We sat at the back of the bar, isolated from most bargoers. I stared down at the four shots laid out before me.

I was a complete lightweight. I learned early in college that I could not drink with anyone. My drink limit was one, and my shot intake was half a shot before I started behaving like a hoochie who hadn't been touched in almost a decade.

I didn't want to act out, but I didn't want to answer questions.

Why was there peer pressure going on here?

This was meant to be a fun night out. Now we were playing drinking games with the hot broody fireman who viewed me like the bane of his existence.

He vexed me. So, so very much.

Selena and I were on one side of the high table, and they were on the other. Nathaniel hadn't looked at me since we settled into our seats, and I could sense he was uncomfortable.

Clenched jaw. Tight shoulders. Hard-set eyes were cast onto the table.

It was ridiculous just how observant I was when it came to him.

"Right, kids. We all know the name of the game. You are asked a question. If you choose not to answer, you drink. Suppose you answer that you don't drink. We keep asking 'til everyone has taken all four of their shots," Xander explained, and I just felt my whole stomach twist. I had promised to take myself out of my comfort zone, but this was...beyond.

Could I get drunk in front of Nathaniel? But the bigger question here was, why did I care? This was meant to be my "living for me" era. I should not put anyone else's view of me before my own.

I stared down at the colorless liquids.

Here we go.

"Firecracker?" Xander looked at Lena. "You ready."

"Do your worst incubator." She threw him a smirk.

"How many people have you slept with?"

She gave him an incredulous gaze, to which he shrugged. "You are so boring. But anyway, I have slept with no man my entire life."

My neck snapped to her. Okay, that was a blatant lie.

"I don't believe you," Xander said what we were all thinking. "You are telling me that you are a virgin?"

"No, I am not."

"But you just said that—"

"You asked how many men I had slept with, and I told you none because I have never actually fallen asleep with a man. But if you had asked me how many men I have had sex with, I would have told you a few."

Smart girl.

"My turn," Selena smiled and turned her sights on Nate. "Mr. Brooding, time for you to answer. I will start you off easy. When was the last time you got laid?"

Nathaniel glared at Selena, and I could feel his coolness

radiating. This man was either icy cold or fiery hot. There was no in-between with him.

He took his shot glass and downed it like it didn't even burn his throat.

"Right, bud, it's your turn." Xander patted his best friend on the back. "You get to ask Lia the question."

Slowly, he flicked his gaze to me, and my breath caught in my throat.

"Would you ever hook up with Xander?"

Xander sputtered out the drink he had been sipping, and Selena looked at Nathaniel with amusement.

My mouth hung open before I remembered everyone was looking at me and waiting for an answer. "No, I would not hook up with Xander. We are friends."

"You were friends with my brother, but then you hooked up with him."

I didn't expect that to hit me as hard as it did, but I felt it. Not all the way deep, but the hit was enough to leave me feeling some way.

"I made love to him. There is a difference."

He scoffed.

"Something funny?" I asked.

Nathaniel leaned back in his chair, his broad shoulders flexing slightly as he set his sights on me. "How many men have you been with after my brother?"

"It's not your turn to ask a question."

"It's zero, right?" He continued. "It's zero because no man would be dumb enough to touch you with a fifty-foot pole. It's a wonder how my brother survived six years with you. God knows it would have driven me to insanity."

His words stung—this time, they hit harder.

"What is your issue with me?" I stood from my chair. "Ever since I got here, you have been nothing but a total ass to me. What have I done to you that warrants your shitty ass behavior? Is it about Jacob? Because if it is, I can assure you the man ended it with me. I wanted him to stay, but he wanted out."

I stared at the gorgeous man wanting him to say something. Anything at all. But instead, I got silence and a nasty glare.

"I need some air. Don't follow Lena."

I walked away from the table before anyone could stop me. The sting behind my eyes intensified, and I felt like I had gone back seven months. The heaviness in my chest just wouldn't let up.

As I exited the door to the cool Chicago breeze, I let out a heavy sigh. I leaned against the wall and looked at the dark sky without a star.

There were very few things I missed about Braven Bay, but one of the things I did miss was the starlit skies. There was too much light pollution in the city for me to see them here.

I heard the door open, half expecting to find Selena, but I was met with an angry Nathaniel. His nostrils were flared, and his chest heaved up and down like a caveman.

"What do you want now?" I spat. "I'm pretty sure you have said all you needed to say for today."

He stormed over to me, and I would be lying if I said his heated gaze didn't cause a shudder to run down my spine.

"What are you doing here?"

"What?"

"In this city. In my city. What are you doing here? One minute I am living my life, and the next, you are here fucking shit up for me all over again?" He ran a frustrated hand through his hair.

"You are not making any sense at all. What do you mean I'm fucking shit up for you all over again? I don't even know you. You understand that. I met you ten times in all six years I dated your brother, and you didn't talk to me even then."

He paced around, looking more and more frustrated. "I knew you!"

I stopped, completely stunned. "How?"

He just stared at me with a blank expression on his face.

"It doesn't matter."

I was tired of his constant hot and cold that drove my head crazy. He could never just pick a damn side.

I stepped toward him and stabbed him with my finger.

"It doesn't matter? You act as if you hate me, and then the next second, you are coming in like a superhero. It all matters because of what you are doing to me! Messing with my head with all this confusion. Why don't you like me? What is your issue with me?"

We were practically in each other's faces now. Neither one of us wanted to bend for the other. I had been the one to yield every additional time, but not today. I would not let this one go. I was going to stand firm and stand up for myself.

"You want to know what my issue with you is?"

"Yes!"

"You're standing here breathing, and she isn't!"

"What?"

"You…you are…" his voice trailed off. "Damnit, you are everywhere. All I can think about is you, and it is frustrating."

He closed the remaining distance between us. There was barely but a whisker of space between us. His hand moved to the side of my face. My breath hitched in my throat when his skin contacted mine.

"You are consuming me."

Then he did something I was not expecting at all. He closed the distance between us and captured my lips in his.

All consuming. Hot. Demanding.

That's how I could describe the kiss. These are all the same things I would use to describe Nathaniel. His kiss was scorching, almost like a branding of some kind.

At first, I stood perfectly still, completely immobile. But his lips continued to coax mine.

He was teasing, taunting, and willing me to move with his rhythmic dance. And so, I did. I moved my lips with a push and pull that could only be felt.

And I felt him. I thought of him right down to the very depths of my soul.

My nerves fired away as the electricity passed from his body to mine and then back again. The atmosphere erupted into a million and one little sparks of fireworks all around us.

My back hit the brick wall behind me, and I gasped.

He took this chance to plunge his tongue into my mouth and kiss me senseless until my entire brain turned to mush.

One moment, this man was devouring me; the next, I felt the cold Chicago air hit me, and his warmth left my body.

My eyes fluttered open in a complete daze of lust and passion. The cloud was hazy, but I saw a stoic-looking Nathaniel through it.

It then hit me what we had just done. My whole heart plummeted to the floor.

"Nate…" I started, but the man turned on his heel and walked down the sidewalk without glancing back.

I was left standing at the front of that bar, confused, heated, and felt like I had just committed one of the most significant crimes in history.

8

AMELIA

I had not seen nor heard from the man who kissed me impetuously and left me on the street. It was infuriating how he had just crossed that line and walked away.

No explanation. No apology.

Just one big smooch on the lips and then gone.

But what annoyed me more was that his kiss had left me wanting, no, yearning for more.

In all my years of life, I had never been kissed like that. I had kissed three men my entire life; he was the third.

He had burned me with his kiss. The kind of burn that ended up warming you from the inside out.

I wanted more of it. It was addictive. Like a harmless drug that had me hooked, I felt that if I didn't get my next fix, I would implode.

I had made great use of my fingers the past few days. But even as I would find myself teetering to the edge, I never saw the happy ending because I was…stuck. I was stuck with him circling in my mind.

His eyes, his calloused touch, his scent.

It was like I had committed it all to memory. I had dedicated him to memory and didn't know how to feel.

Selena had looked at me oddly when I returned to the table. My lipstick smudged, but she didn't ask me bout it. She let me be, which I was grateful for.

A few days later, I had a new client to prepare for and went out to get supplies. My arms were filled with flowers, baskets, and fairy lights.

I waited in the mirrored elevator until the door dinged open on my floor.

The stuff in my arms was blocking my vision. I didn't see the person just outside the elevator until I ran them over… again…and sent everything I had tumbling to the floor.

"I am so sorry. I wasn't looking—oh, it's you. We got to stop meeting like this," I smirked shyly, looking at the man I had been silently simmering with over the past few days. I dropped to the floor and picked up the flowers and the baskets.

To my surprise, the giant brooding man got down and helped me with my stuff. Instead of handing it to me, he looked at me, waiting for me to start toward my apartment.

"You want to help me?"

"Unless you want to carry these all yourself and risk knocking over another innocent bystander."

I rolled my eyes. "You could see my line of sight was blocked. You could have moved over."

"You bulldozed me down, yet again. I didn't have enough time."

That was true. I had nearly knocked him over, but that was because I was reeling from thoughts of him and the fact that I hadn't had a decent orgasm in days. Every time I tried, I couldn't. It was his fault.

"Fine, follow me." I led the way to my apartment.

I was hyper-aware of his closeness to me. The man was like a tall tower, for crying out loud. His scent of spice and leather filled my nostrils, and I was instantly taken back to that night.

The way he had held me and the way my body had just set on fire after his touch.

Dammit. This was not the time to be thinking about him this way. This man was not my friend, and I was mad at him. I needed to stay mad at him.

I unlocked the door to my apartment and let him go in first.

"You can just put them on the counter over there."

He set the flowers he held on to the counter, and I did the same.

I then turned to the tall, brooding man, unsure what to do next. I wanted to ask what the hell that was at the bar the other day. But I also knew that my chances of getting an answer were slim.

"Well, thanks. You can go now." I shifted my weight from foot to foot.

He stood in his place still as stone.

"You can go," I said again. "Your services are no longer required here."

He stared at me with those eyes. They were like swords piercing right through my entire chest. The air in my lungs suddenly evaporated, and I was left reeling.

The space between us crackled to life just like it had that night at the bar. That pulling feeling returned, and I felt my entire body buzz with excitement.

There was something about him that just awakened me. There was something about him that ignited all the dead and broken parts of me.

I hated how my body reacted to him when my mind

knew better. I knew better than to feel this way for someone like Nate. He was like a sin.

Dark. Tempting. Forbidden.

If people could be drinks, then he would be a dark bourbon. Once you drank him in, you would taste his bitterness. It would bring your senses to life and air into your lungs. And then the burn followed if you decided to take him in. A scorching kind of burn that you always remembered. It was the kind of pain that went back in for more. But only if you were brave enough to retake him.

Bourbon was not simply a drink you fell upon, like vodka or tequila. It sought you out. Bourbon was only for those who could stomach its bitterness and burn.

It was not for the faint of heart. So now I wondered to myself why I wanted to try it.

One brother had already scarred my heart. Why would I put myself in the line of fire again, only to be destroyed by the same bloodline?

"Why did you kiss me?" I filled the silence with my voice.

I watched his features harden.

"You have acted nothing but mean and cold toward me from the moment I met you. Yet you punched a guy harassing me, and then you kissed me a few hours later. It doesn't make sense to me. We live in the same building, and Xander and I are friends, and likely our paths will cross. So, for the sake of peace, I want to squash whatever issues between us. I won't ask about what you said that night. But I want to know why you kissed me?"

He stood there still as stone, not answering me as I had expected him to. But when I thought he would do nothing but stand there and say nothing, he opened his mouth.

"I didn't know I was doing it until I did it," he said. "It

was a mistake on my part. I am sorry for crossing the line with you like that. It won't happen again."

I let out a sharp breath. I don't know why the word 'mistake' stung more than I thought it would.

"Okay." I crossed my arms over my chest. "Can we call a truce now? I moved here to avoid all the drama and the stress, not to get involved in more."

I held out my hand for him to shake. He looked at it for a few seconds before taking my hand.

"Truce," he agreed.

Those familiar sparks that had pricked my skin that day returned. I quickly ripped my hand from his and took a small step back.

"I should get ready for my client."

"Client?"

"A first-time mom. She's bringing her baby girl in for a photo shoot."

"You're a photographer?"

I nodded. "Yep. It started more as a passion project, and I discovered I could profit from it. So I monetized my passion. I strictly do newborns and pregnant women, but I think I could expand further."

"Why them specifically?"

I shrugged. "I don't know. I've kind of just had an affinity for babies and pregnancy. I like the idea of new life and new hope. It's stupid, I know, but it's—"

"It's not stupid," he interrupted me.

My heart jumped.

Something passed between us within those few seconds, and we stared at each other. The air buzzed with something electric. But as soon as that moment came, it was interrupted by the blaring of his phone.

I jumped a little, and he dug his phone out of his pocket.

"I better take this." He started for the door. With his

hand on the knob, he paused before he turned back to look at me with a hint of warmth in his eyes that I didn't see there before. "See you around, Amelia."

"Bye."

And with that, he left me with many emotions and a wetness that I was becoming too accustomed to between my legs.

Great.

9

NATHANIEL

The girl was in my head. Amelia had me in this vice that I could not get out of.

I shouldn't have kissed her, but I did. I shouldn't have allowed myself to get close to her, but I did.

When I had almost laid everything out there for her, the look in her eyes had my chest tightening. I could see the confusion and hurt on her face. She didn't deserve that.

She was barely six then, and from what I remembered at the hospital, she had no idea what had happened. But still, I could not separate her from the blame of the night. She had been there and survived—the same way I had. But it had been her fault. At least, that was how my brain viewed it.

"You look like shit," Xander said from beside me as we walked to our cars. "You need to get some rest."

"No shit." I hadn't gotten a lick of sleep yesterday, which was never good on a 24-hour call, but shit happened. "Where are you off to? Meeting another escapade of yours?"

"Nope. I'm meeting Selena at a café up the street. She's trying to convince me that vegan life is the way."

"Wait, Selena? As in Amelia's crazy best friend?"

Xander smirked. "That is the one. The girl has a mouth on her, but damn, I love it."

"You are trying to hit that?"

"Yes," he shrugged. "I'm always up for the challenge. Besides, after that night at the bar, I need to show her I'm not just a guy who is only into sex."

"But you are a guy that is only into sex."

"But does she know that?"

"Yes." Clearly, he hadn't been paying attention that day at the bar. "She called you an STD incubator, or did you miss that part?"

"That was a joke."

I shook my head. My friend was either delusional or just dumb. Possibly a combination of the two. The girl Selena was a firecracker, and she was not to be messed with.

"I don't think you should mess with her, Xander."

"Says you." He scoffed. "Besides, I haven't done anything with her, and I doubt she will even let me touch her. But I am up for the challenge. If she shoots me down, then she shoots me down. But at least I would have laughed while getting shot down. The girl is funny as shit."

"You have the strangest taste."

"I like what I like."

I walked over to my truck and pulled the handle open.

"Hey, Nate?"

I paused, waiting for him to continue.

"And you be careful."

I looked at him, confused about what he meant by being careful.

"Amelia," he explained. "I don't know what the hell is going on between you or what she did to piss you off, but she is a good person."

I grunted my response and got into my car. Xander went his own way, heading to his date.

I sat in my car for a while, just thinking over everything.

My head was a cluster of emotions. I wasn't thinking clearly, and it was starting to seep into other areas where it had no business.

That day when I apologized to her, I had lied. I knew what I was doing when I kissed her. I knew exactly what I was doing. But the problem was that it should have never happened. She was my brother's ex-girlfriend. A girlfriend I was sure that he was going to get married to.

My phone buzzed in my pocket, and I dug it out.

"Speak of the devil." I saw his name flash across my screen and hesitated for a split second. My brother and I were not close, but I loved the guy. He was my flesh and blood. But I couldn't deal with him being so close to her. But now she was close to me, and I was self-combusting.

I slid my finger across the screen, and I answered, "To what do I owe the pleasure of you calling me little brother?"

"Hey, Nate." He sounded tired and worn down.

Usually, my brother was a lively little shit who talked too fast and animatedly. This was a little weird for him to sound so mellow.

"What's wrong?"

"Nothing," he yawned. "Just went out last night and got back home late. No big deal."

"It was a Tuesday last night."

"I know," he said.

"Why are you going out on a bender on a Tuesday night? Don't you have work?"

"I took some personal days off. I needed to rethink my life a little bit." The silence was on the other end of the line as I waited for him to continue. "I've had a lot on my mind that I've been dealing with, and it's been messing with me... pretty bad."

I took a sharp intake of air.

"What do you mean?"

"I don't know, man. Maybe it's like some quarter-life crisis that I'm dealing with. Or maybe it's the breakup. All I know is that my head is spinning, and alcohol seems to work until it doesn't."

My chest tightened at his words. "I thought we learned from Dad that booze does nothing for you but hurt you and those around you."

"I know," he groaned. "I know that. But I just needed to take the edge off. I didn't want to go down Dad's path, but I felt so…alone."

"What happened to your girlfriend?"

This was a question I had wanted to know for a while now, but I just hadn't figured out how to ask it. We weren't close enough for me to randomly ask about Amelia out of the blue. Especially when he thought I hated her.

"I broke up with her." There was something in his tone that raised a lot more questions in my head.

"Why?"

Silence.

He didn't answer me for what seemed to be a minute, if not more.

"I didn't think she was what I wanted anymore. She was just so…stuck. At least, it seemed that way in my head. She always followed me around like a lost puppy. It was like she didn't have a mind of her own. She tried to intertwine everything we did. It felt like she was taking away my identity."

Why did I find that hard to believe?

"She was always on my case about marriage and babies and settling down and, I don't know, I guess I just panicked. I'm only 22. How can I introduce life into this world when I don't have my shit together? How would that work? But she kept pushing and pushing, and I guess I just snapped. I wanted out."

I thought back to the time in her apartment when she had told me that she wanted to have babies of her own one day.

New life. New hope.

"Did you ever tell her you were feeling that pressure?"

"No," he finally admitted after another long pause. "I didn't want to upset her. So, I just kept telling her soon. I told her that she would be the mother of my kids, but I didn't know if it was immediate like she wanted."

It made sense why she had been so upset.

She had felt like she was promised this world that he had painted for her and even confirmed for her. Then, one random day, he broke her heart and told her he wanted out.

I understood my brother's side. I was the same way. I didn't want anything serious. I didn't want to be tied down right now. I was happy with my job, my life, and my city. I didn't need anything or anyone else coming in and ruining that.

But I also understood her side. The girl longed to be a mother. I saw the look in her eyes when she talked about her work. She was passionate for sure, but she yearned for that experience herself.

"Had she always wanted to be a mom?" The question was random, especially coming from me, but I couldn't help but want to know more about her. There was something about her that intrigued me.

"It's all she ever wanted. She only went to college to appease her dad. But she always knew that being a stay-at-home mom was all she ever wanted. She wanted the full dream. White picket fence, carpool, and yearly family vacations."

It suited her. That life she so desperately yearned for. It was who she was without a doubt in her mind.

· · ·

"She's gone now, in any case. I don't know where she is. But when I stopped by her house, I found it empty. Mama Gertrude, the woman next door, said she moved out months ago."

So, he didn't know where she was.

It would have been the perfect opportunity to tell him that she was now my new neighbor and she was in Chicago, but I decided to keep my mouth shut. She would have told him if she had wanted him to know where she was.

"Okay," he breathed out a heavy sigh. "Enough about my failed love life. I called to tell you that Dad wants you home for the holidays. Thanksgiving is in a couple of weeks."

"No." My response was immediate. "You know I don't want to return to Braven Bay, and besides, Dad hates the holidays. Why the sudden change of heart?"

"He said that he had something to tell you."

"Then he can call me. I don't want to set foot in that place ever again. I told both of you when I left, and I'm telling you now; I'm done with Braven Bay."

"It's your home, Nate."

"Chicago is my home now." My tone left no room for discussion. "Look, I just got off a long shift and need to rest. Tell Dad I'm sorry, but I can't. He has my number, and he knows where I live. If he needs a plane ticket, I can get it for him. But I'm not coming back to Braven Bay. Not now or ever."

"Fine," he clipped. "But just call him when you get the chance. He…wants to hear your voice."

We hung up the call, and I leaned back against the headrest.

My father and I have had a somewhat strained relationship since my mother's passing. He said he didn't blame me for the accident. But I knew that deep down, he did. It was how he would look at me at times. I saw it in his eyes.

55

'It should have been you.'

He had never outright said it to me, but I knew he thought it. If he could, he would have traded my life for hers. But I didn't blame him. He was right. I would have changed my life for hers too.

With that last thought, I revved my car to life and headed home.

10

AMELIA

My lungs complained as I completed the last few blocks. I had pushed my legs much harder than I had been anticipating. But I needed to clear my head. Today was one of those bad days that I was having.

But to be fair, I had done it to myself. I was the one who had gone digging into his social media.

Yes, I had caved and stalked my ex on social media. The man was living it up completely and utterly fine without me. I didn't know how to feel about that. On the one hand, it hurt like hell; on the other, I had this sadness that I couldn't fully hold.

Jacob was smiling like he was actually smiling. The kind that reached your eyes and everything. It got me thinking that I may have been the cause. Maybe there had been some absolute truth to his words, and I had been the cause of him being so unhappy in his life.

Jacob had been my entire world. He was my whole existence. His presence alone made me happy. It hurt me that I was the one thing sucking away his happiness.

I pushed my legs harder, trying to run from the voices of the past, but they just kept getting louder and louder.

I could feel the sting behind my eyes. Besides that, all I felt was this overwhelming pain in the center of my chest.

I came to a grinding halt at the entrance of my building and doubled over with my hands on my knees and my chest heaving heavily.

I needed to leave the past in the past. It was behind me. I was a different person now, and so was he. It didn't matter if he was happier without me. I was more comfortable without him. For the first time in a long time, I was choosing myself.

When I straightened up, I saw a familiar figure walking my way. He had his bag slung over his shoulder, and his entire body looked stiff.

When our eyes connected, his steps faltered briefly before continuing.

My first instinct was to dash inside, but we had called for a truce. We were no longer on warring sides anymore. We could come together as two grown adults.

"Morning." My voice sounded too chipper, and I internally cringed at that. "You're up early."

He came to a stop in front of me. There were about two feet of distance between us, yet I inhaled his spicy scent that made its way toward me.

"I just got off shift."

"Oh," I said and shifted between my feet. "You do the night shift now?"

"It was a 24-hour shift."

My eyes nearly bulged out of their sockets. "24-hour shift. That's…that's wild."

"Not really. I have the next 48 hours off duty to get them back."

I made a face. "I couldn't imagine being on shift for 24 hours."

"What? You have a strict night routine that you need to follow?"

"I do, smart ass." I crossed my arms over my chest. "My head must hit the pillow at exactly 9:30 to get the correct rest. More rest means fewer wrinkles when I'm older."

"I don't think that's how it works, but more power to you."

Would you look at that? Nathaniel Cane and I were being civil. Who would have thought?

I thought this guy was a giant prick only a few days ago, and now…he was half a decent guy. It was refreshing.

"Morning run?"

"Yeah. I needed to clear my head a bit, and I—you're bleeding." I grabbed his chin; I stepped closer, turning his head to expose the oozing blood scratch on his neck. "What happened?"

His hand came on top of mine. Then, I realized just how close we were to each other.

"I must have nicked myself when I was getting over the fence when we got a call last night."

Tiny little tingles traveled up and down my arm, my body hyper-aware of him. "I can help you out. Come to my apartment." I was surprised I could even formulate coherent words at this point. It felt like there was this chaotic storm attacking my senses.

"It's fine. You don't have to do that."

"Just come." I detached my hand from his, finally able to breathe once I stepped back. It was like my system short-circuited when he was close. "I have a first aid kit."

I led the way, and he followed wordlessly behind me. The entire time I felt the buzz in the air. The electricity crackled around us. That was what this man did to me.

We walked into my apartment, and I took him to my bathroom, where I ordered him to sit on the toilet seat.

I made quick work of getting my supplies and began cleaning the wound. Honestly, it was more of a scratch, but the blood oozing from it had been worrying.

I angled his head so he was facing far right so I could better access his neck. I was between his legs, and my boobs were right in his face.

Thank God the Chicago Fall was chilly because I would have been in a sports bra or tight tank instead of a sweatshirt. But still, this closeness to him had me feeling all flustered again. I could feel the heat reaching my face, and I only prayed that my cheeks didn't turn red. But with my luck, I was probably as bright as a tomato in season.

I dabbed the alcohol-dosed swab onto his wound, and the man hissed, grasping my wrist in his large hand tightly.

I froze instantly. Those little, tiny sparks now have shock waves roaring through my veins.

"Umm…" I cleared my throat. "Sorry. I need to get it clean."

His forest green eyes were set on me. His mouth pursed thinly. His breathing came out ragged and a little labored, but I didn't know if that was from the swab or… me.

Was he as affected by me as I was by him?

This man. This gorgeous human specimen had bulldozed his way into my life in a way I had not seen coming. I had promised myself that I would avoid him. I had promised myself that I would keep a safe distance between us. But now, having him only mere millimeters from me, temptation flowed through my blood.

I wanted to feel his searing kiss again. I wanted to be tasted by his skilled tongue. I wanted to know how he truly felt. Was he rough? Gentle? I didn't just want a taste. I wanted to devour it all. I wanted to devour all of him.

I was walking into dangerous territory. The truce had

only been there for a day or two, and now I was already trying to get into the man's pants.

His hand moved from my arm and came to rest on my hip. Heat poured into my center, and I did not doubt it was wet. I was likely drenched.

All this man had to do was look at me, and I would be a goner.

"Amelia." The way he said my name only fueled the hungry fire inside me. His hand tightened on my hip, eliciting more shockwaves throughout my body.

My hand came to the nape of his neck, pulling his head closer. I stared down at him, his green eyes molten with desire and passion.

The air thickened with the tension that had followed us from the moment we saw each other. And now we were here. Alone. Hungry for each other.

I don't know who moved first, but our distance suddenly closed.

My fingers played with the tiny hairs on the back of his neck, brushing against his skin as it prickled with goosebumps.

His other hand came to my waist, drawing me closer until I was flush against him.

I continued to lower my head toward his lips. My restraint was all but gone.

Soon, we were but a whisker's distance apart. His hot breath fanned my face. The pleasure pooled into my core. I was wet with desire.

I only needed to lean forward to capture my lips in his.

A loud blaring filled the air, and I jumped away from him as his touch burned me. My phone buzzed in my back pocket, breaking the bubble we had found ourselves in.

The music continued to blare as I stared at the man I had

promised myself that I would not touch again. But here I was, feeling him all over again.

I had been so close to caving in.

His green eyes bored into mine as he could see right through me. I felt naked under his eyes. Overly exposed and vulnerable.

I needed to say anything to cut through the embarrassment that hung in the air. I did not doubt that my face was red or that my eyes were as wide as saucers.

"I need to go and get a cantaloupe…from the store." That was all I could come up with. Really? "Umm, I'm sure you can show yourself out."

Like the coward I was, I didn't even wait for him to respond. I just ran out of there like the room was on fire.

I didn't stop until I was safely inside the elevator heading downstairs to get a cantaloupe I did not need. I wouldn't even say I like cantaloupe. It wasn't good. I always thought when I was little that it was a wannabe watermelon.

I leaned against the elevator wall and groaned at my stupidity and embarrassment.

I had almost kissed my ex's brother. Hotter older brother, but that didn't matter. What did matter was that Nathaniel Cane was off-limits. That was a line that I could not afford to cross again.

"I need to stop thinking with my vagina," I muttered to myself as the doors to the elevator opened, and I walked out.

Operation Avoid Nathaniel started today… I would stick to the number one rule this time. Don't kiss or touch Nathaniel Cane. How hard could it be?

11

AMELIA

I took a few snapshots of Claire rubbing her belly. The woman was stunning, even though she had said that she felt like she looked like a walrus. I told her that she was wrong. Pretty golden hair, olive skin, and striking hazel eyes with shades of blue. Her features were soft and delicate, almost like a fairy. Or that had more to do with the ethereal-looking dress she wore. The woman was dressed like a forest princess with a leaf crown to match, but that had been what we were going for.

"You are so stunning, Claire." I smiled, to which she responded with her soft smile, but it was the kind that didn't quite reach her eyes. "Take a look."

I got up from the floor and walked over to her. I showed her the pictures I had taken. She was beautiful. Even with the light streaming in from the window, casting this golden light on her skin was just perfection.

My favorite picture was of her rubbing her swollen belly and looking down at it with so much love and adoration. But when I looked up to gauge her reaction, she had silent tears streaming down her face.

"Claire? Are…are you okay?"

She blinked, coming out of her reverie. "I'm sorry. These hormones have been doing a number on me."

That wasn't why she had tears, and I knew it. There was a kind of sadness that followed Claire. I could see it in the way that she moved. It clouded her eyes when she stared off into the distance.

"We can take a break if you need to." I set my camera down on the counter and turned to her. "I have some ice cream that I have been dying to bust open."

She brushed the remaining tears from her eyes. "I'm lactose intolerant."

Oh crap. "How about some chocolate cake?"

A teary smile graced her elegant face. "That would be nice."

"You can just have a seat on the couch."

She rubbed her belly. "Thank you."

She made her way to the couch that I had pushed to the side for me to make my DIY set for her shoot. Working out of my studio apartment was a bit of a drag, but at least I didn't need to rent a space. I was still starting out.

I walked over to my fridge and pulled out the chocolate cake I had made yesterday. I had one of those depressive days and needed a little pick me up. Sugar was always an excellent way to heal a broken heart.

I grabbed two forks and returned to my client, who hummed gently to her belly. When I set the cake down, her eyes lit up.

"Chocolate is my favorite."

"Mine too." I cut a slice for her and myself and sat beside her. "How many months?"

"Nearing seven months. It feels like I've been pregnant for a year." She took a forkful of the cake before closing her eyes and humming her appreciation, "Oh, my God. This is amazing. Is this store-bought."

I couldn't help the little sense of pride that filled my chest. "Nope. Homemade."

"You're kidding. You must give me the recipe."

"Of course." I smiled, continuing to eat the cake.

"Are you new to Chicago?" Claire asked.

I nodded while taking another bite.

"Yes. I just moved here after a terrible breakup. I felt like I needed a change. Staying in my hometown would have been too painful for me. My boyfriend was the golden boy. So, seeing him everywhere and seeing everyone's pity, I just... I couldn't do it. I had always wanted to pursue photography professionally, but Jacob, my ex, always said it wasn't sustainable as a career. I guess he was right, but after the breakup, I thought, screw it. I felt proud of myself for taking the next step."

"Breakups are hard." A sense of loss in her tone caused me to look at her. I could see the sadness swimming in her eyes. But it wasn't shallow or an 'I'm hurt' kind of sadness. It was that kind of sadness that consumed all parts of you. It took you hostage and didn't let go. This kind of sadness placed you in a bottomless, dark pit that was impossible to escape.

"Claire?"

"Hmm?"

"Are you okay? Like, for real? Are you coping okay with everything?"

I knew she wanted to lie to me. She tried to force a smile, but then it fell. Tears pooled in her eyes. "I...I just..."

I dropped my fork and moved close to her on the couch. "Is it okay if I hug you?"

She nodded, letting out a low sob, and allowed me to hug her. I held Claire in my arms while she let out all the pain she had been holding in. I knew this cry. It was a tired and worn-out cry that could only be felt deep within the soul.

I don't know how long we stayed, but by the time she had pulled away, my shirt was stained with tears, and her makeup had smudged.

"I'm so sorry. I messed up your shirt." She gestured to my top, but I waved her off.

"It's just a shirt. My concern is you."

Her lips quivered again, but she didn't break out into tears. "I just feel overwhelmed. From the baby to the new house and everything else in between. I don't know how I will handle it all alone."

She stared down at her stomach lovingly as any expecting mother would. But from the moment Claire had walked in, I could see the dark cloud that followed her.

"My brother told me not to come to Chicago, but I was young and thirsted for adventure. I should have just stayed in Braven."

My ears perked at the mention of my hometown. "Braven? As in Braven Bay?"

She moved her teary eyes to me. "Yes. You know it?"

"Know it? I was born and raised there."

"You're kidding? Me too!"

I looked at her face closely. I was trying to place those delicate features in my mind, but I came up blank.

"What part of Braven did you stay in?"

"Oh, in Calloway Creek."

Okay, that made sense. She had grown up on the other side of town. She was from the more affluent part of town. They weren't millionaires. Their houses had land, and the private school, Braven Academy, was there.

"So, you moved here alone?"

"Yes. At first, I was a little scared, but the city suited me.

It was this breath of fresh air away from Braven. I had always felt so trapped there. Like I was suffocating."

I knew that feeling, but it had been numbed by my love and devotion to Jacob for years.

"Oh," she jumped, making me worry.

"Are you okay?"

"Yeah," she said and smiled. "Little guy is just active today. I think he likes your cake."

I stared at her stomach in awe and wonder. When she saw my expression, she grabbed my hand and placed it over her belly. She moved it around until she came to the side when I felt the little kick.

My eyes widened in amazement. "Oh, my God."

There was a life in there. I mean, I knew the whole concept behind a child. But truly realizing that her body was creating and housing this little life inside her was remarkable.

"I know. It makes it all seem real now. I only wish Ethan were here to see it."

"Ethan?"

"My husband." She smiled sadly. "He died in a car crash the month after I found out we were pregnant. He was my best friend and the man I thought I would love for the rest of my life."

Tears brimmed her lids, but she quickly batted them away.

"I have been trying to come to terms with everything with the pregnancy and Ethan but…" her voice trailed off.

"It's unfathomable," I said.

"Exactly." She gently caressed her stomach. "I met Ethan when I moved here. It was one of those whirlwind-type romances. We dated for three months and were married by month four."

Her voice was laden with sadness and pain. She loved this man.

"When we got pregnant two years later, I was scared out of my mind. I had just lost my job, and Ethan had just started at a new firm. But he said we would manage, and I believed him. Ethan had this way of reassuring me and making me believe whatever he said."

My heart broke for her. I couldn't imagine moving through pain like that. My heartbreak now felt like child's play compared to what she was going through.

"I'm so sorry. Do you have any family here?"

She shook her head. "My mother was an addict and died a little over three years ago, just before I met Ethan. I never knew my dad because my mom refused to tell me. But she did say that he was some hot shot in New York. I didn't have any brothers or sisters, or at least any I know."

"What about Ethan's family?"

"He doesn't…I mean, he didn't have any family. He was an only child and was raised by his grandmother. She passed away when he graduated college."

"And what about your brother?"

"He's working on relocating to Chicago for a few months until I can get on my feet with the baby. He found a job at this law firm."

I reached for her hand and squeezed it in mine. "I know this may not be worth much to you, but you also have me for whatever you need. I mean it. I work from home, and I happen to love babies."

A low, quiet sob left her lips, but she pushed it back down. It broke my heart at how tired and worn out she seemed. This was supposed to be one of her happiest days. Instead, she was out here dealing with grief and the stress of soon becoming a single mom.

"You would do that for me?"

I nodded. "Of course."

"You have the kindest heart, Amelia." She pulled me in for a hug before she jumped back, rubbing her swollen belly. "Oh, sorry, he's kicking in there today."

She moved my hand again to meet his little kicks, and I felt him again. The little guy had some power in those muscles.

I had never felt something so… unique in my life before. There was a tiny little human life in her belly. A human life that she had created with the person that she loved. It was only a shame her partner wouldn't get to witness it.

"He's feeling strong," I beamed at the mother-to-be.

A sad expression took over her features. "Much like his dad."

I just kept making her sad. I needed to be more careful about what I said.

Tears welled in her eyes, and I cursed myself internally for returning her to the memories of her dead lover.

"More chocolate cake?" I offered a sweet distraction. Thankfully, she took the bait and went with it.

Claire and I talked like we were old pals catching up for hours and hours. We ordered some food and binge-watched the first few Game of Thrones episodes.

By the time she was leaving, she seemed a little lighter, and her eyes didn't seem as downcast.

"Come over anytime you want, Claire." I hugged her tightly. "I mean it. I'm just a phone call away if you need anything."

When she pulled away, she had a beaming light on her face. "Thank you, Amelia. What you did for me today…. words can't express how grateful I am."

And just like that, I made a new friend in Chicago.

12

NATHANIEL

I wouldn't say I liked Fall. It was the season when all these ridiculous holidays popped up. The first one begins with Halloween. It was an excuse for society's weirdos to express their inner strangeness. It was also the time of year the station got overly busy because people ended up doing some dumb shit that found them in trouble.

But this year, Xander and I had Thanksgiving off, meaning we would spend the day at his house. I didn't want to return to Braven. His parents and siblings were all out of town.

Xander had two older brothers. Yes, he was the family's baby, which, to be quite honest with you, explained his childish tendencies. His older brother Matthew was a surgeon at Chicago General. And his second brother, Caden, was a hotshot tech guy in Silicon Valley. He made an app during his senior year of high school and sold it for over 10 million dollars. If he wanted to, Xander could have quickly become one of those stuffy guys on Wall Street. The guy was a super genius when it came to numbers. But he was passionate about being a firefighter and following in his grandfather's footsteps. But that never stopped the guy from making a killing in the stock market. The man had money, but he rarely spent it. But his home was an indication of just how well off he was.

He lived in a penthouse deep in the heart of the city. It wasn't the most lavish penthouse, but with oversized floor-to-ceiling windows, light hardwood floors, and new white furniture, this place reeked of money.

I sipped on my friend's expensive whiskey and looked at the skyline. It was yet another gloomy day in Chicago. The clouds had rolled in, and I did not doubt that the temperature had dropped drastically.

"You're brooding," Xander knocked me out of my reverie. He came up beside me with a glass of whiskey in his hand. "If you keep frowning like that, your face could freeze, and then you will have no chance of ever finding a woman."

"I don't want a woman," I said as I side-eyed him.

"Oh really?" Here we go again. "Last I checked, you had your tongue down a certain brunette's mouth not too long ago."

I clutched onto my glass, hoping I wouldn't have to punch my friend in his home.

"Come on, man. I can see it on your face. This girl has you all wound up, and you don't know how to deal with it."

"I don't know what you're talking about. That is Jake's girl."

"Correction, she was his girl. And last I checked, you and your brother aren't even close. The girl has the hots for you like you have the hots for her."

"Just drop it, Xander." I downed my drink and went to pour myself another. "And when is the food going to get here? I can't keep drinking like this on an empty stomach."

"Should be here any second now."

As if he summoned it himself, the doorbell rang.

"Oh yeah, I invited Amelia and Selena to dinner." Then he rushed down the hallway to answer the door.

What the hell?

He could not be serious right now.

I had been trying to avoid this woman like the plague. It was bad enough that I lived a few doors down from her, but now I needed to endure this dinner with her.

I hadn't seen her since she ran out on me from her bathroom. If she hadn't been the one to break away first, I would have kissed her again, if not more. And I wanted more. Dammit, I wanted it all.

The thing about me is that I am a greedy asshole. I want it all. I need it all. That kiss outside the bar was a simple taste. Now, my only goal was to have it all.

I heard the voice in the hallway, but they still needed to round the corner. My heart fluttered in my chest, something it had never done before.

The footsteps drew closer and closer, and then she appeared. She wore a long white dress that hugged her figure, and her dark brown hair cascaded down her back. She was a true vision in white.

Her lips were split into a smile as she listened to Xander and Selena bicker with each other like children. I had no interest in their conversation. My sole focus was on Amelia.

When she finally turned her head in my direction. The smile slipped from her face, her lips parting ever so slightly.

The atmosphere shifted to something more electrified and alive. Her eyes connected with mine, and I froze. In this lighting, they seemed bluer than they did green. Her face had the slightest hints of makeup, just enough to highlight her beauty—and my God, she was beautiful. She was a far cry from the girl she had been that night. Scared. Alone. Bloodied.

Immediately the bubble that had encased itself around me popped. I moved my gaze to the two bickering adults, sipping my dark liquor to suppress whatever confusion was ripping through my body.

"Okay, let's call a truce. It's Thanksgiving, Lena. Bring it in." Xander opened his arms and moved to Selena, who was backing away with a scowl etched on her face.

"You called my pie deformed and radioactive." She threw the pie she was holding in his face. "I put effort into this thing, dammit."

"Are you sure about that? It looks a little—ow! That hurt, Selena."

"Good." The woman smiled evilly at my best friend. She then moved her gaze to meet mine, and her smile widened. "Well, if it isn't the little 'Ice King.' You still got a stick up your ass?"

Amelia nudged her friend with a warning look and a hushed scold.

"Selena," I drawled. "Always a pleasure to be in your presence."

What had Xander done? There was no way I would get through tonight without the aid of some suppressant.

This was going to be a long night.

After the bickering had stopped and the food for dinner arrived, we all gathered around the table, waiting. We were only staying because Xander had to take pictures to send to his family group chat and prove that he made the food—a lie.

"You know they will never believe you made all of this,"

Selena said and leaned into her chair. "Do you even know how to boil water?"

Xander gave her a deadpanned look and took the last of his pictures before settling into his seat beside me. Amelia sat across from me, and Selena across from him.

Amelia had not looked my way once.

"Okay, time to be grateful." Xander clapped his hands together. "Hold hands, everyone."

He had to be kidding.

"I said hold hands." He stared at all three of us, his hands stretched out, waiting for us to do as he wanted us to. "Humor me, people."

Reluctantly, we all did as we were told and joined hands. My system was shocked when my hand met with Amelia's. When I looked at her to see if she was affected by my touch as I was with hers, I saw nothing. Her face was completely passive and unreadable, apart from the slight parting of those soft lips.

"Okay, now I think it would be nice if we all went around the table and said what we were grateful for this year."

There was no way in hell that I was doing that. This wasn't a Hallmark movie.

"I will start," Selena cleared her throat, turning to her best friend. "I am most thankful that my best friend finally found her voice and started living for herself. I know the circumstances that brought you to Chicago were not ideal, but they gave me you again, and I couldn't be happier."

They shared a moment, Amelia's eyes brimming with unshed tears, that wall of hers crumbling to the ground.

"Me next," Xander spoke up. "Although I would love to be sappy and cute to Nate and say I'm thankful for him, I'm not going to. So, instead, I will say I'm thankful for this moment right here. To old friends and new. Nate?"

I didn't even know what to say. There wasn't much in my life to be thankful for. I lived the same old life and did the same things every day. There was no notable standout—apart from Amelia. She was the only thing that was different in my life. She wasn't even mine, yet she consumed me like she was.

There had been odd days when I had found myself missing her face or yearning to talk to her. I couldn't tell you how many times since that day I had almost gone up to her door or finished what had started between us.

But I could say none of those things out loud unless I wanted to risk losing my brother and crossing the extensive red line I had drawn.

"Pass."

"Oh, come on," Selena booed me from her seat. "Are you telling me that there is not one thing you're grateful for? Not one thing that made your year this year?"

My gaze cut to Amelia for a split second connecting with her eyes before shifting my focus away.

"Nope."

"Wow, how sad."

"Selena," Amelia hissed at her friend. "That's not nice."

"What? I'm only stating facts."

"Can we move on, please?" I didn't have time for this, and the food was getting cold. "Amelia, go."

My voice startled her, causing her to jump slightly, her hand clutching harder onto mine. The electricity pricked my skin, and the hairs on my head stood up. This woman was going to be the death of me.

"Oh yeah…umm…what am I thankful for? I guess, leaving home. I had grown up in Braven Bay and felt safe and secure all my life. For a long time, I thought it was all I wanted out of life: a white picket fence house, a husband who adored me and my children. Any outside dream seemed…impossible. I didn't allow myself to dream too big. But now, I guess, that's all changed. I'm free to follow my passions and what my heart desires most, even if it is one of the scariest things I have ever endured."

This piqued my interest. I knew next to nothing of her life in Braven Bay after I left, but from what it sounded like, my brother had been a class-A asshole.

"Okay, let's eat," Xander announced.

Dinner moved quite quickly, surprisingly. The conversations were kept light. By the discussion, I mean between Xander, Selena, and Amelia. I ate in silence and observed everyone.

It was a skill I had picked up when I was in the Marines. You needed to speak less and watch more. You learn more about the people around you and your surroundings.

When we were done, Selena and Xander ran to the store while Amelia and I stayed behind to clean up. I knew that Xander only made that arrangement so he could get Selena alone, and I was not a man who wanted to stand in the way of the mission of my best friend. But I didn't want to be alone with Amelia, especially after the bathroom incident.

I dried the plates while she washed and hung them on the rack. Leave it to Xander to break the dishwasher and make me do his manual labor.

"I can feel you are staring," I said as I turned to look at Amelia, who stood at the sink with her hands in the water. "Say what you want to say, Amelia."

Heat covered her cheeks before she turned away.

"Sorry." She replied shyly.

I placed the plate I had been drying onto its shelf before leaning against the hard granite of the tabletop and looking at her directly.

"Don't do that," I continued. "Say what you want to say.

You have been staring at me for the last half an hour. So out with it."

"Umm…" She was hesitant to say anything at first, but then she found the courage she needed somewhere in her head and turned to face me.

"I don't know how to act around you. I am trying to figure out whether you hate me or not. And how we should interact. One night we kiss, and then the next, you tell me to get out of your face. You are also my ex's older brother, which is…against some rule somewhere?"

"Are you asking me or telling me?" I arched an eyebrow.

"Telling." She shook her head, completely flustered. "Look, all I'm saying is this," she gestured between us, "is messing with my head. You're in my head. Everywhere I turn, you're there. It's like you're freaking Casper, a ghost sent to haunt me."

I couldn't help the slight tug on the ends of my lips. Seeing her all frazzled and flustered was cute. Her eyes darted everywhere, but she refused to meet me.

I placed the dish towel down, crossing my arms over my chest.

"I'm haunting you?"

This time her eyes flitted to me, and her blush deepened when she saw the amusement on my face. "You know what I mean."

"I don't. Enlighten me."

"Enlighten you?"

"Yes," I shrugged. "I'm a little slow, so you may need to help me."

"Nathaniel."

"Amelia."

"You're infuriating."

"And you're confusing."

"How am I confusing? I said what I said, and I meant what I said."

"I don't understand what you said, so you're confusing."

I don't know how we got there, but we suddenly faced each other with only a few inches of space between us. I could feel the heat radiating from her body. Little sparks of electricity moved between us.

My body was wide awake now. All I could feel and sense was her.

Her sweet vanilla and strawberry scent filtered into my nose. My eyes moved down to her parted, plump lips, her low and breathless gasp filling the silence.

The ever-growing need to touch her increases with each passing second. Her body called to me in ways I could not form into words. It was carnal and unhinged.

My hand moving on its own accord, I brushed the stray piece of hair that had fallen out of place. When my fingertip contacted her skin, instant shock waves of electricity shot throughout my arm.

She must have felt it because her eyes dilated, and her body leaned more toward me. The tension grew thicker, and the heat that moved throughout my body now headed down to my groin.

"Nathaniel…" she said my name almost like a silent plea. She leaned into my hand, her eyes closing at the contact. When her eyes opened again, I saw the heat and the desire. I saw the need for this forbidden fruit that hung before us.

We were teetering on a very fine line.

Danger and destruction. Passion and desire. Temptation and sin.

I don't know who moved first, but suddenly the distance between us was closing. Inch by inch, we moved, tentative, scared, and curious.

My eyes had flitted closed, waiting to feel her soft lips on mine again.

"We're back!" Xander's voice caused me to jump away from her like I had been burnt. "And we brought more alcohol!"

I looked to Amelia, who had already turned from me and busied herself with the remainder of the plates.

13

AMELIA

I was playing with fire, and I was about to get burnt. I had gotten lucky a few times, but my favorite pass time these days were challenging fate.

The man had gotten under my skin in ways no one ever has. Seeing him from across the hallway damn well nearly sent me into cardiac arrest.

Last night I had watched him from the corner when I was coming in from my run. He was carrying groceries, and I kid you not, my whole body was excited that this man was carrying groceries into his house.

I was losing it.

So, what does one do when they are borderline losing it? They head to an arts and crafts store to go and buy a stress relief coloring book.

As I was sitting sifting through the various sections in the store, I found my mind drifting back to the man I was so desperately trying to forget.

That moment in Xander's house was a close call, and I knew we couldn't afford moments like that again. It wasn't safe for either of us. But I so desperately wanted a moment like that to arise again. I wanted to feel his touch and his gentle hands on my skin.

I was not shy to say that Nathaniel Cane had plagued my mind since the first kiss. I had tried everything: my fingers, high-pressure water. I had even purchased a new vibrator. I had gone to great lengths to try and get this man out of my mind.

Maybe it was the fact that I hadn't had sex in almost a year now. Jacob and I had stopped being intimate three months before we broke up. In hindsight, I should have seen that as a sign that he had detached, but I was a fool and in love with a fool. Now, here I was, pining after his older brother.

I had no shame.

I groaned, flipping through the coloring book I was thinking of getting.

"Who am I kidding?" I slammed my head with the book. "What am I going to do? Color the horniness out of me?"

I heard a gasp beside me, and my neck snapped to the left to find an older woman giving me a disapproving look.

My cheeks blushed. "Oh no, I didn't mean…."

"You kids of today have no shame," she scolded me, waving her paintbrushes in her hand. "Get cleansed!"

She waddled off to the till, leaving me to drown in my mortification.

I moved away from the aisle I was in and went down to the pencil color section. This was what I got for talking out loud. Next time I need to keep my big mouth shut.

I wanted to know if my day could get any worse, and then it did.

It all happened so fast that I don't remember all of it. But one minute, I was trying to choose between a pack of 50 or

25 colored pencils, and then I heard the explosion before being thrown back by the force of the large burst. My back hit the wall opposite the section I was in. Then it all went black from there.

14

NATHANIEL

"**E**ngine 42! Ambulance! Explosion on Deerfield and Main." The alarm rang throughout the entire section.

Everyone rushed to the brigade and put on our gear. The truck stormed out of the house and headed to the explosion site. Adrenaline pumped through my veins as we prepared for what could be a messy situation. These were the moments that I lived for. My senses became laser-focused on the task, and my body flexed as I prepared for what lay ahead.

"And here I thought this would be an easy day." Xander put his helmet on beside me. "Time to be a hero, I guess."

He always said that every time we left the station. He had this weird superstition that something terrible would happen if he didn't say it. I didn't believe in all that, but I have to say, with every call we took, we never had one casualty.

"Okay, listen up!" Brian, our lieutenant, commanded our attention. "I need everyone ready to go on this. I don't want anyone taking any risks. It's a crafts store with some highly flammable stuff in there. I need clear radio and clear communication. Understood?"

"Yes, sir!" we all replied.

When we got to the scene, it was exactly what I had expected. Flames engulfed the roof, and smoke leaked through the windows. Shards of broken glass scattered all over the floor.

People raced out of the building coughing as they broke through the gloom of smoke surrounding them.

"Nate, Xander, and Daniel head inside to check for survivors. Franklin, Abby, and Josh set up a perimeter and get these people as far away from this place as possible. Johnny, man the hose. We need to get this fire under control before this whole thing blows."

After we got our orders, we all dispersed.

"Don't be an idiot, Xander." I put my gas mask on while walking toward the flames.

"Don't try to steal my thunder, Cane." He laughed, putting his mask on before heading into the burning building.

As soon as I entered past the flames, my instincts kicked in. I did my best to search through the smoke for anybody who needed help to make it out.

"Fire department, call out!" I yelled as I moved through the smoke. I tried fine-tuning my ear to hear any meek or low responses. "Fire department, call out!"

Broken pieces of wood and glass lay on the floor. Pencils and papers littered on the ground that I walked on.

I turned the corner expecting not to see anyone, but then I paused when I saw a body lying unconscious on the floor. She had her back to me, but I could see her chest as it rose and fell.

I rushed toward her. "Ma'am, are you okay—Amelia?"

I turned her body so she lay on her back. Soot covered her olive skin, but even with all the specks of dirt on her face, I could still tell it was her.

"Amelia! Amelia, can you hear me?" I slapped her face a few times, but she was unresponsive. "Dammit, Amelia…please."

I wasted no time placing her on my shoulders and approached the exit. I could hear the creaking of the wooden beams above me. I knew that they were mere seconds from giving out.

I tightened my hold on her and picked up my pace. Blood rushed past my ears as I tried to see through the smoke to get us to safety.

"Nate, you need to get out of there," Brian said over the radio. "Building is about to give out."

"Moving," I said back. "Shit."

I moved around all the fallen debris until I finally left the exit. I had made it two meters when another explosion sent me flying to the ground. Amelia fell from my grip and tumbled to the ground beside me. I immediately covered her with my body to keep any flying debris away.

When I pulled back, I looked down at her face. Her eyes were still closed, and she didn't look like she was breathing.

"Meg!" I yelled for one of the paramedics to get over to where I was. "Amelia? Amelia, can you hear me?"

She was unresponsive.

"Cane, you need to move," Meg knelt beside her. "I got it. Damon, start an IV."

Meg and Damon got to work, but I stayed rooted in my place, looking down at her.

"Nate, move!" Meg's voice was distant, almost like she was underwater.

Memories of that crash came flooding back into my body. The rains. The shattered glass. And the blood. All the blood that had mixed in with the rainwater.

"Nathaniel." This time it was Xander who dragged me to my feet. "You need to let them work on her."

85

I was still in a daze between the present and the past.

I watched as they placed her on a stretcher. My eyes never left her face once. All I could do was stand there. Unlike the last time we had found ourselves here, I could do nothing to save her.

Xander's face came into view, his lips moving, but I couldn't understand his words. My eyes stayed trained on Amelia. All I could think about was that little girl I saw crying in the backseat with her face all bloodied.

"Nathaniel!" Xander's voice broke through my clouded haze.

"Yes?" I cut my eyes to him, the dread seeping deeper into my bones.

"We can meet her at the hospital, but we need to get this shit sorted first, okay?"

I nodded, the words locked in my throat. I watched the ambulance head off to Alvaro Memorial. There was nothing I could do for her now. My head was needed where I could be helpful.

I pushed down the internal chaos currently filtering into my bloodstream. I had a job, and I would worry about outside things later.

She would be okay. She had to be.

15

NATHANIEL

When everything was under control, we returned to the station for clean-up. After scrubbing and showering, I walked out of the house to my truck.

The entire way there, my heart was in my mouth. My mind was coming up with the worst possible scenarios.

I asked Meg, and she said that she was okay. She was stable when they dropped her off at the hospital, and she had even been conscious, but only enough to answer her questions.

I tried to run it back about a hundred times what her body looked like on the gravel. I hadn't seen any noticeable bleeding. But what if she had internal bleeding? What if she had hit her head when the first explosion happened?

My foot pushed harder down on the gas, sending me flying down the Chicago roads like a madman.

By the time I got to the hospital, my mind was spiraling. I moved my legs as fast as I could to the reception area. Alvaro Memorial was a great hospital and regarded as one of the best in the country, but I knew that I would not be able to calm myself until I saw her.

"Amelia Rose Carter. She came in after the fire at a crafts store. She is twenty-two and brunette." The woman in scrubs just blinked at me like I was talking gibberish. "Are you hard of hearing or something?"

She scowled at me. "I don't appreciate your tone. That is not how you speak to someone."

I ground my teeth together in annoyance. "Look, I just need to see Amelia Rose. She was taken here by a colleague of mine, and I—"

"Nathaniel?" A man I had not seen in a very long time walked to the front desk. "It's okay, Anne. Let him through. He's a friend of mine."

The nurse, Anne, gave me one last glare before turning her gaze to Buck. "Teach your friend to have some manners, Bucky."

If I weren't in such a panic, I would have questioned the nickname she gave him, but my mind was solely focused on Amelia.

"He's a little slow, Anne." Buck winked at the girl, who blushed and returned to what she had been doing before I got there—nothing.

Buck walked me past the waiting room doors and into the ER. He stood at an impressive 6'4" and looked as big as he did when we were both with the Marines. Albeit, he had shaved off the unruly beard he used to sport and decided to replace the baldness on his head with some blonde hair.

"As I live and breathe, Nathaniel Cane." He smacked the back of my shoulder. "What has it been? Five, six years?"

"Seven. You look good, Buck."

He smiled. "Leaving the war zone will do that to you. I didn't know you were in Chicago."

"I moved down here after my last deployment in Syria.

Look, Buck, I don't mean to be an asshole, but I'm looking for someone. We can catch up some other time, but right now, I need to—"

"This way, asshole. She's in trauma seven." He rolled his eyes. "And what do you mean? Being an asshole is your default setting. It's why I liked you so much."

Buck walked me to the room in the ER. Every room in the ER was separated from the others. Sliding glass doors with curtains behind them acted as blockers.

"Here you are," he stopped just a few feet from the room. "I'm the one treating her. She had a little smoke inhalation, and we gave her some oxygen. She's a little spooked, but other than that, she's medically fine."

I nodded, the large lump returning to my throat. "Thanks, Buck."

From the small gap in the curtains, I could see her lying on the bed with her eyes cast to the ceiling. She didn't have the oxygen mask on anymore and still had soot residue on her face, but at least there was some pink on her cheeks.

"Girlfriend?" Buck looked between me and the room that housed Amelia.

"No."

"Wife?"

I shook my head. "She's…" I didn't even know what to call Amelia and me. We were far from friends, and there was no chance we could ever be more than that, so I settled with something more neutral.

"She's important."

"Hmm. I see." I could see the wheels turning in his brain, trying to piece together what I wasn't actively saying.

"I have other patients, but you owe me a drink."

"You got it, Buck." I rubbed my hands against my work pants and entered Amelia's room.

She was dressed in a gown, and her hair flowed down her

backside. When she heard me enter, her eyes moved from the ceiling to the doorway.

Her face went from shocked to confused to shocked again.

"Nathaniel? W-what are you doing here?"

Hearing her voice diminished all the dread that had poured into me hours ago. Watching those hazel eyes look at me with so much…life in them washed away all the anxiety that had locked itself tightly in my muscles.

I swallowed hard, trying to clear my throat of any obstruction. I didn't know why I was so nervous. It wasn't like I hadn't been with her alone. But this was also the first time I was seeing her since Thanksgiving.

"I came to check on you." My voice came out thicker than usual.

Her eyes held mine.

"How did you know?"

"I'm the one that got you out. Do…do you not remember?"

She shook her head. "The last thing I remembered was picking out a coloring book, and then…it all went black. Then when I opened my eyes again, I was here."

"I see." The air thickened in the room, the tension increasing the longer I stayed rooted in my place.

Now that I had seen her, I could leave. There was no reason for me to stay.

"Glad to see you're okay." I cleared my throat. "I'll get going now."

"Do you need to? I know you may be on duty, but could you? Stay, that is." Her voice was so soft and meek. I could see this ordeal's toll on her—the fear that swam behind her eyes, the tension locked in her body tightly.

"Okay."

"You know you don't have to stand over there, right?" The ends of her lips tipped upward. "I won't bite."

She may not bite, but she was dangerous to me. Being near her had proven to be a risk. Yet, my feet moved toward her without a second thought.

"Why were you at a crafts store?"

Her lips parted into an oh shape, and her cheeks took on a light pink shade. "Oh that, well... um. Why does it matter?"

"Well, for one, you are currently in a hospital bed. Not to mention the fact that you don't paint or draw."

"Says who? I have many talents that you may not know about. May I remind you that you barely know me?"

"That may be true, but I had also seen your artwork when you were in high school. Your work left much to be desired."

"What?" She squeaked, "I will have you know I won an award and an art competition my freshman year."

"It was a participation award," I deadpanned. "You are great behind the camera. I would say phenomenal even, but actual art is not your forte."

She tilted her head to the side. "You've seen my pictures?"

"Just your earlier stuff for your senior year project."

Her eyebrows pulled together, "But how? You weren't even home at the time. Weren't you deployed in Syria?"

She was right. I was. But Jake had posted a picture she took of him, and curiosity got the better of me. I wanted to see what she was all about; the girl was talented. It was no wonder she was already racking in clients.

"I was, but Jake sent me some of your work to update me on his daily life."

I may have imagined it, but I could have sworn that I saw a little glimmer of disappointment wash over her. But she quickly corrected herself, masking whatever was going on in that little head of hers.

A moment of silence passed between us. The air thickened more and more with each passing second. The buzz that moved in every nerve in my body was maddening.

"Thank you, Nathaniel," She whispered. "For saving my life."

Thump. Thump. Smack. My heart pounded heavily in my heart like a bass drum.

"You're welcome, Lia." Her nickname rolled off my tongue like butter.

A single breath escaped her lips.

Every molecule of oxygen evaporated from my lungs, leaving me breathless. She was covered in dirt, her hair was unbrushed, and she wore a hospital gown. But she never looked more beautiful in my eyes.

My eyes moved from hers down to her lips between her white teeth. I wanted nothing more than to loosen her hold on her lips and claim them as my own.

These carnal thoughts were the same ones I had tried to suppress for months, but all they had done was feed my hunger and need for her.

For months I had told myself that she was not mine to have. That she was off limits. But at this moment, staring into her eyes like I was, I felt the possessiveness take siege of my heart.

I knew navigating things with her would be tricky, given how intertwined our pasts were. But now I realized just how screwed I truly was.

NATHANIEL

"Nathaniel?" Her voice came out like a breathless prayer between us.

"Yes?"

"Tell me something real about you."

The question was so out of the blue that I had to blink a few times to understand if she had said that.

"Something real?"

She nodded slowly, holding my gaze. "Something no one knows. A fear of yours. A comfort you seek out when the world gets heavy. A truth you're scared to say."

The last one had some hidden message behind it, but that was something I wanted to avoid unpacking today or ever.

"I'm not scared of anything."

"That can't be true." I knew she wouldn't believe me. "Everyone is scared of something."

"Not me. The worst fears of my life came true when I lost my mother. Now everything else seems so...pointless after that."

It was true. The pain I experienced when I lost my mother was unlike anything I had ever felt in my entire life.

It was this crippling kind of pain that left me frozen in time. I couldn't look back because the memories were too painful, but I couldn't move forward due to the guilt that weighed heavily for survival.

"I'm scared of thunderstorms," she confessed. "I was in a horrible accident that took my mother's life and another person in the other car. It was pouring down rain in Braven Bay. I don't know exactly how the accident occurred, but from what I know, my mom lost control and hit an oncoming car. I was six at the time this all happened."

It was that night. She was talking about the time both of our lives changed forever.

"I woke up in the hospital. I don't remember much of what happened in the accident, but I remember someone pulling me like a hero. The doctors said if I had been left in the car for any longer and not attended to, I would have died on the spot. I've feared storms ever since. They remind me of the day a person I loved so dearly in this world was taken from me. I wasn't even able to go to the funeral. I was in a medically induced coma for at least a month before awakening. And when I woke up, I didn't know and didn't want to exist in the new world I had fallen into.

Even at the tender age of 6, I knew I would never be the same. But for my father's sake, I pretended all was well because I knew he was grieving, and he couldn't worry about the both of us." Her voice grew thicker with emotion. The slight crack tugged at something in my chest. "Looking back at it now, I probably should have said something instead of feigning happiness. Maybe I wouldn't have made many choices that led me here today."

One of those choices concerned my brother, but I would not ask her about it. This topic was still so fresh for me, even though it had been nearly sixteen years since the accident killed both of our moms.

I had replayed that night repeatedly in my head. She was also wondering if she could have done anything differently. Would they have both lived if her mother hadn't been so careless?

My mother wasn't supposed to be out on that bridge that night. She had only come to get me from a party I was told not to go to. She had worried that if I drove myself, I would have crashed and died. But it turned out to be her instead.

So many things would have changed if people had made slightly different choices that night. Maybe my mother would have lived. Maybe her mother would have lived.

Amelia began to speak, breaking me from my what-if scenario sorrow train.

"Maybe that's why I stayed with your brother as long as I did." She let out a humorless laugh.

"I don't doubt that I loved Jacob. He was my first everything. But now I realize that I used him to cushion my pain. I used him to make those hollow days seem more bearable … after a while, he just became a part of my daily routine. Maybe that's why he broke up with me. He knew he needed to chase after more in the world, and I guess I do too."

Her words hung heavy in the air. Her eyes had glazed over, teleporting her to a faraway place, and when she finally blinked, she moved her gaze from her hands to my face. Her features softened, and her hand reached for mine.

Instant shock waves rolled throughout my body at our contact, and it took every ounce of willpower I had not to react.

Time stopped then, and all that existed was her and I. The bubble encased us in the singular defining moment.

Flashes of Thanksgiving filtered into my mind. We had been so close. I wanted to. I relate to giving in to all my desires and to caution. There was no one here to stop us. There was no barrier anymore.

I cupped the side of her face, brushing my thumb against her cheek. She closed her eyes, leaning into my touch. When she opened them again, I could see the deep seeded desire and want in them.

She wanted this just as badly as I did.

Come on, Nate. Give in. Allow yourself a taste of the forbidden fruit just one more time.

"Nate…"

I could not stay strong and away from this beautiful creature much longer.

Just then, someone pulls open the curtain.

"Amelia Rose, what were you thinking going to—oh, Nathaniel? What are you doing here?"

I jumped away from Amelia like she had caught fire.

Déjà freaking vu.

It had happened yet again. Except this time, it was Selena who had come to stop whatever would have transpired between the two of us.

"I was just seeing if Amelia was okay."

Her eye shifted between me and her best friend. She didn't even bother to smother that knowing grin from her face.

"I see."

"I should get going. They need me at the station." I gave them a curt nod before leaving the room and going to the parking lot.

That was twice now that I had fallen into this situation with Amelia. Or was it three? First, she abruptly ran. Then, twice we've been interrupted.

I couldn't help but notice the tiny flicker of disappointment that gnawed at me. If only her friend had come thirty seconds later, would I have finally kissed her again? I shook my head, trying to rid myself of these obscene thoughts.

I couldn't want Amelia. She was a no-go area for me. I needed to keep my senses when it came to her. But the annoying thing was that Amelia could break down your walls without even trying. So, it then begged the question, why even bother building a barrier if she would tear it down?

17

AMELIA

Christmas was just around the corner, and I had spent the first part of the festive season cooped up in my apartment.

After the hospital, Selena interrogated me like I was Pablo Escobar. She called my bullshit repeatedly when I told her nothing was happening between me and Nathaniel. But the more I refuted her, the less I believed it myself. There was something there between the two of us. There had always been something there from the moment I saw him the day I moved in.

It was something so raw and untamed. It was carnal in its nature and unpredictable. Usually, all those things would have scared me, but they did nothing but excite me.

That was what Nathaniel did to me. He excited me. Maybe it was his dominating aura, but something about him pulled me toward him. It was like a siren call that only our two hearts could hear.

Suppose he had consumed me before he had now officially undone me. The man was there when I closed my eyes and the first thought when I woke up. I had tried to chase down orgasm after orgasm, but I was sourly disappointed whenever I got close to my release. I couldn't even pleasure myself in peace anymore.

The thunder roared, shaking my glass window. I jumped back, clutching my coffee mug in my hand.

A storm was coming in, meaning I lived with level nine anxiety. I had cuddled up on my bed with tea and some Netflix on my laptop. But even that wasn't helping me to calm my nerves.

I didn't like these storms. Usually, I would take some melatonin and sleep through it, but I was out of the sleep aid and was not about to go out into the pouring rain to get more.

The thunder roared again, and I whimpered a little, trying to calm my racing heart. No matter how many years had passed, my mind still took me back to that night. The only thing I remember was talking to my mom about what theme I wanted my birthday to be and then black. The sound of glass shattering and metal colliding will forever be engraved in my brain.

I had "Stranger Things" playing in the background, but that didn't even help.

My phone buzzed on my side table. It was probably Selena checking in. But when I swiped on the screen, I realized it was not Selena.

Nathaniel Cane: open the door.

I read it over three times to ensure I didn't see things. But that was him.

I pulled the blanket off my body and went to my front door. When I opened it, I found the 6'3" beast of a man on the other side holding a brown bag and two coffee cups from Sally's.

"Nathaniel." there goes my heart again. "What are you doing here?"

"It's storming outside," he answered.

"Okay?"

"Can I come in?"

The logic was screaming that I shouldn't do it. Being trapped here would only put us back in situations like Thanksgiving and the hospital. That possibility alone was reason enough for why I moved aside for him.

Whenever he entered my apartment, he practically filled the whole place up. It wasn't a tiny space, but his presence was so large that it demanded your attention, and you couldn't help but move with him.

"I brought the chocolate fudge cake you like from Sally's." He placed the brown bag on the counter. "And some chamomile tea with oat milk."

"You brought two?" I walked over to the two to-go cups.

"No." he grabbed one of the drinks. "This is a hot chocolate for me."

"Oh."

His eyes remained glued to me. Those forest green eyes that reminded me so much of the countryside in Braven Bay stared at me with the kind of danger that should have sent me running for the hills. But all it did was cause more blood to rush down my groin.

All the man had done was look at me, and I was already wet. But to be fair, he had been on my mind these past few days. And I had been holding back the floodgates when chasing down my orgasm.

Hold it in. Hold it in, Amelia. I had to repeat to myself repeatedly to keep myself from jumping the poor man.

"Uhh…" my voice filled the silence. "Thank you for…this."

I picked up the cup and sipped on the chamomile. It was still piping hot, meaning he had gotten it not too long ago.

"When did you get this?"

He sipped on his drink, his eyes staring at me over the rim. "Ten minutes ago."

My eyes bulged out of their sockets. "Are you crazy? There is a storm, and you went out there? Do you know how dangerous that is?"

"I'm aware."

"You could have gotten hurt, Nathaniel."

"Unlikely, but okay." The man leaned against the granite tabletop, his eyes still holding me.

"This isn't a joking matter, Nate."

"Am I laughing?" He wasn't, but I could see in his eyes that he was amused, which only upset me.

"Don't do that again." I sipped on my chamomile.

"What? Go and get you comfort food to ease your anxiety, or come keep you company during a storm?" He set his cup down and inched closer to where I stood in the kitchen. "Because if you want me to go, I can, sweetheart."

The name caught me off guard. So much so that the grip on my tea tightened, squeezing the top contents of it out and spilling onto my hand.

"Shit," I hissed.

Nate sprung and took the cup from me before taking my hand and running it under cold water. He stood behind me, pressing his front into my back while washing my hand. The pain that had burned my skin was now forgotten, and suddenly I was utterly hyper-aware of everything that involved Nate.

His fresh musky scent of spice and leather filled my

nostrils. The heat from his body rolled onto me, blanketing me in warmth.

"You're very absent-minded."

"You say things that catch me off guard," I mumbled.

With him being this close, my brain was practically mush. It was even hard to formulate a coherent thought. All I could think about was how good his body felt against mine.

He affected me greatly. More so than I thought he could, and it unnerved me. I always loved the control and knowing exactly how things would go. But with him, it was always so chaotic and unpredictable.

I shouldn't have liked it, but I did. His chaos was intoxicating.

Wanting to test the waters, I pressed my back into his front ever so slightly. I felt his body tense up, and his hand was still underwater.

Electricity sparked on the surface of my skin as I repeated my action, wanting to get a genuine reaction from the man behind me.

My hormones were ruling me.

I had this sizeable, engulfing blaze burning in my core for weeks. And I knew his touch was the only way to extinguish it.

Nathaniel lowered his head, bringing his lips right by my ear. His free hand rested on my hip, pulling me firmly against him.

"Don't start something you can't finish, Amelia."

I gasped, feeling his growing length behind me. "I have every intention of finishing whatever this is. The question is, do you?"

A low growl rumbled from his chest. He turned me in his hold, pressing my back against the granite.

"You're playing with fire, Amelia Rose." He was barely

holding on. His eyes darkened with desire, the hardness of his length pressing deeper against me.

"Burn me, Nathaniel."

He didn't even hesitate.

He smashed his lips onto mine, searing with his kiss. The kind of burn hurt so good it was like ecstasy.

There was no turning back now.

18

AMELIA

Our lips meet aggressively. Our mouths begin to fight for dominance. Neither one of us was trying to give up control.

He lifted me, so I sat on the granite. I was then reminded that I was wearing little boy shorts that were a little shorter than I would typically wear, and the tight tank I wore left little to the imagination. No wonder the man had looked like he wanted to devour me. I had practically bared myself to him unintentionally.

His kiss was far better than I had remembered it. Maybe it was the build-up that had led to this moment. Or perhaps it was that this time we knew there was a rush to it all. We weren't sneaking about or finding little stolen moments in between. This was just him and I—two adults devouring each other like teenagers.

We pulled apart, gasping for air. Our breaths mingled together in wanted passion.

I was lost in the cloud of lust, passion, and everything in between.

Nathaniel cupped the side of my face, gently brushing his

thumb across my quivering bottom lip. His pupils were dilated from the sheer desire that floated between us.

"Nathaniel," I gulped. I wanted more of this. I liked everything he could give me but didn't know how to ask for it without sounding like an overly aroused weirdo.

"Nate." His voice was gruff and coated with thick emotion. "Call me Nate, sweetheart."

"You said only friends can call you that."

The sides of lips tipped upward slightly into a gentle smile. "Nathaniel is far too formal for what I'm about to do to you."

My heart jumped, threatening to leave my ribcage. "What are you going to do to me?"

The smile slipped from his face, the danger in his eyes screaming at me. "I'm going to ravage you, sweetheart. I plan on ruining every other man for you."

He placed a sweet kiss on my lips before pulling away. Then he moved to my cheek and kissed me there. Then he moved to my forehead, kissing me softly. After that, he moved down to my nose and softly kissed the tip.

His hands rested on my bare thighs running up and down my skin. Little tiny sparks moved up and down my skin. The last bit of fragile resolve left me, and I broke. I wrapped my arms around his neck, pulling him toward me with a different kind of hunger.

Our lips came together once more. My fingers dug into his hair, tangling with the soft locks. I tugged on it gently every so often to be rewarded with a moan and a growl.

I ground my hips into him, wanting to quell the hunger that had riddled my body.

I moaned into his mouth, wanting more of him. I needed to feel him in all areas and as much as possible.

He lifted me into his arms and guided us to the bed,

where he threw me down, breaking our kiss. I lifted onto my elbows, watching as he stripped to his boxers.

Good. God.

I had seen this man's body before, but he was still a sight. Chiseled torso. Deep v-line drawing a perfect map to the one thing I desired most.

"Want to take a picture, sweetheart? It will last you longer."

"Don't be so full of yourself, Cane. It's unbecoming."

He winked with a devilish grin. His eyes moved from my face to my chest to my legs. Slowly he brought his gaze back up again, but the smile that had painted his features was gone. In its place was this smirk that had my insides jumping with excitement.

"Up," he ordered me. "I want you to remove all your clothes for me, sweetheart."

"No, please…" I teased him by batting my eyelashes slightly.

I only did it to rile him up a little, which worked.

"Don't make me strip you down myself, Amelia. Up. Now."

I did as I was told.

As I stripped off the minimal layers I had on, I held his gaze. I could feel the wetness building between my legs. My lips were swollen and throbbing in need of some much-needed attention.

I stood straight, completely bare and naked, in front of him.

The adrenaline pumped into my body like never before. I was ready for him. I had been ready for him for weeks.

He stepped toward me, closing all the distance that existed between us. His hand reached between us, his fingers running up and down my swollen lips, causing me to let out a string of moans. I moved against his fingers wanting him to go a little lower, and moved inside.

"You're so wet, Amelia." He wound his free arm around my body. Our bodies pressed firmly against each other. "All this for me, baby?"

I couldn't speak as his fingers dipped lower and teased me at my entrance.

"Nate, please..." The fire was too harsh for me to withstand anymore. I was done trying to fight it. I needed release. I needed to feel him.

"Tell me what you want." He kissed my bare shoulder, teasing me again. This time he dipped one of his fingers in before withdrawing completely, causing me to whimper. "Tell me what you want, Amelia."

His two fingers slipped inside of me with ease. I arched into him, my knees just about holding on.

"Tell me, baby." He moved his fingers with a painful kind of slowness. "What. Do. You. Want."

"I want...I want you to fuck me." It slipped past my lips, trying to hold myself steady with how his fingers moved in and out of me.

"What was that? I didn't quite catch it."

"I want you to fuck me," I said, increasing the volume of my voice. "I want you to fill me so deep that I forget my name."

He removed his fingers and unwound his arm from my waist. I whimpered at the loss of contact, to which he only smiled before kissing me like he owned every last inch of me. When he pulled away, he was out of his boxers.

I stared down at his impressive length, my mouth going completely dry.

I felt he was big, but I never anticipated him to be this big.

"On your hands and knees," he commanded.

When I didn't move, he turned me, placing me in the bed and smacking my ass hard, earning a moan from me.

"When I tell you to do something, sweetheart, you listen. Am I understood?"

I nodded, but then another slap fell on my ass, sending shockwaves through my bloodstream.

"Words, Amelia. Use your words."

"Yes," I breathed.

He came up behind me, his length teasing my entrance. "This isn't going to be gentle, Amelia. I don't know how to make love, but I do know how to fuck, and I will fuck you until all you can think about is me inside of you."

I licked my lips, the anticipation gripping my throat. "Less talking, more fucking, Nate."

He laughed, the sound burrowing into my chest and gripping my heart tightly.

"Such dirty words from such a pretty little mouth."

Without warning, he plunged himself inside me, filling me all the way. It had been a while since I had last felt a man inside me. It took me a moment to adjust to him. He was much bigger than what I was used to, but he felt so good inside me.

"Nate." I moaned his name like a plea. "Oh, my God."

"You take me so well." He slid out of me before slamming right back into me. "Like you were made for me."

He was the ice to my fire. Two opposite worlds collide in harmonious chaos. He was indeed my undoing.

Thrust after thrust, I met him at every movement. He pushed into me, and I moved back onto his cock. He drew me closer and closer to my release. My body heated with all the movement, sweat beading my forehead as we went at it like dogs. He flipped me on my back and put my legs on his shoulders, thrusting deeper and filling me even more.

. . .

The only sound that could be heard in the room above the thunderous boom from outside were his grunts and my moans, all tangled up.

"You feel fantastic, Amelia."

"Yes, yes, right there."

He was relentless.

Skin-to-skin smacking, my arousal coating his thick cock as he moved in and out of me. He moved his hand between us and rubbed my clit with his thumb.

"Oh my God," I hissed at the sheer pleasure that poured into me. His following thrusts could only be described as animalistic and savage. They ripped right into me like never before.

His movements were harsh, deliberate, and core-shattering. He was right. There was nothing sweet or tender about this. This was raw, primal. He was claiming me as his just as he said he would. He was ruining me. But I needed it.

"Nate! Please!" I didn't know for how much longer I could hold on. "I need to come."

A slow hard thrust again sent more shockwaves throughout my body. "You want to come?"

"Yes," I groaned.

Slam. Slam. Slam.

He buried himself deeper and deeper.

"Fine." He raised to his knees on the bed, raising my legs onto his shoulders even higher, angling me just enough for him to take up the last bit of room I had left inside of me. "Come for me, baby."

He was relentless as he pounded into me. But within seconds, I was shattering underneath him, my walls squeezing him tightly.

"Amelia, shit," he groaned, following closely behind with his own orgasm.

We rode out our high together. His lips covered mine

with the small remnants of passion that filtered out of his body.

Our bodies were laden with sweat, my sheets completely a mess. I could only imagine what I looked like.

I wanted the regret to hit me like a truck, but nothing came as I stared at the man who still hovered above me, searching my face as I did his. Those green eyes glistened with a peace I had never seen.

We had just crossed a line today that could not be uncrossed. I had moved into new terrain with him and had to figure out how to navigate it.

Nathaniel Cane was not the kind of man you experienced without a few scars. I just had to make sure I survived whatever came next.

19

NATHANIEL

The rain had calmed outside to a slight drizzle, and the sun had fallen, giving way to the night. Amelia lay beside me, knocked out and satisfied. After our first round of sex, we ate some chocolate cake. She convinced me to try an episode of Stranger Things. But as we lay underneath the covers completely naked, my hand found her wet and ready to go again.

We had gone at it like rabbits. But the real kicker was that I was still hungry for her. Not an ounce of the hunger I had for her had quelled. I wanted more of her, so I took her in every way she was willing to give. We had had sex on the floor, the bed, and her countertops, and I had eaten her out on the table. I had claimed every orgasm and silenced every pleasure-filled cry.

She was so responsive to my touch. As I lay beside her, trailing my fingers up and down her back, she shuddered slightly in her sleep.

We had fallen asleep a few hours ago, but I was cursed with insomnia and could not sleep through the night. So, when I woke up, she was still knocked out cold. I don't know how long I had laid here just staring at her face, but it had felt like no time had passed.

Her cheeks were flushed, and her dark hair unruly, but she never looked more beautiful. I had fought it as best as possible, but the pull between us was too great.

Amelia stirred a little in her sleep, but she didn't wake, so I kept moving my hand up and down her spine. After a few minutes had passed and I was convinced she was still asleep, her lips pulled up into a soft smile.

"You're staring," she mumbled into the pillow. "I can feel it."

"How long have you been awake?" I asked.

She popped her eyes open to look up at me. "Long enough to know you're obsessed with me, Cane."

"Obsessed with you?" I stilled my hand on her back. "Says the woman who kept screaming my name all night."

Her eyes popped open before she ducked under the sheets hiding from me. I let out a soft chuckle pulling the sheet from her face. But she clutched onto that thing for dear life.

"Lia," I laughed. "Let it go."

"No," She squeaked. "I just realized that I look a complete mess, and you were looking at me while I was a complete mess. Turn around."

"I've already seen you."

"Don't care," she held onto that sheet as if her life depended on it. "I need to look more presentable."

I gave one last tug and released the sheet showing her face. She buried her face into my naked chest, to which I just laughed again. She was just too damn adorable.

"Oh my God, look away, Nate."

Her calling me Nate just made my whole day. I loved how it rolled off her tongue, coated with a sweetness like honey.

"You look fine, sweetheart. In fact…" I grabbed her shoulders and pulled her back to look into her eyes. "You look freshly fucked and radiant."

Her blush deepened. "Don't say things like that."

"Like what?"

"You know…"

"I don't know. Please enlighten me, Lia."

She huffed, blowing the strands that had fallen across her face. "You're insufferable."

"True. But according to you, I'm also 'so fucking big I could rip you in two.'"

She gaped at me, completely mortified. "I did not say that."

"Oh yes, you did. You said a multitude of things while you were drunk on sex."

She groaned, leaning her forehead against my chest.

I couldn't help the laughter that bubbled up inside of me. Within the past few hours, I had laughed and smiled more than I had in an entire year. She brought out this different side of me. A side that I had long thought was dead.

I kissed the top of her head, drawing her even closer to me. She felt at peace. Being next to her, the chaos ceased for a few minutes. I wasn't followed by the dark cloud that had loomed over me for years.

We fell into a comfortable silence holding each other. There was no awkwardness or this need to fill the silence. It was just her and I who existed now.

"Thank you." Her voice was merely a whisper, but it might as well have been a thunderous boom in the room's quiet.

"For what?"

"For coming to me during the storm. You didn't have to do it, but you did it anyway."

"You don't have to thank me for being there for you, Amelia. It's not a task for me."

"I know, but I just want you to know how grateful I am that you made the time." The sincerity in her voice made me wonder if she ever had people show up for her. Amelia was a giver and rarely asked for anything, if at all. She was the kind of person who stuck her neck out for other people, even the ones who didn't deserve it.

I tipped her chin upward and captured her lips in mine. Usually, our kisses were hot and demanding, but this one carried more tenderness and sweetness. This wasn't about branding one another. This was simply a comfort—a message saying I'm here for you.

When we pulled away, her eyes were warm with an emotion that was too foreign for me to comprehend fully. So instead of trying to delve too deep into it, I pushed it away.

"So, what happens now?" She bit down on her lips nervously.

"What do you mean?"

"This whole thing between us. Where do we go from here?"

I cupped the side of her face feeling her smoother skin beneath my rough palm. Amelia was my sweetest temptation and deepest desire personified. Now that I had tasted her and felt how she felt around me, gripping my length as she owned it, I could not let her go.

"I want you, Amelia. I know I shouldn't, but I do." She leaned into my touch with the sweetest smile.

"But…," I continued, "I can't give you the fairytale kind of love your heart desires. I'm not built that way. I don't believe in love or happily ever afters. My heart is incapable of it. And I don't want to put you into anything where you feel you must give up parts of yourself to be with me."

She pressed her hand on my chest.

"I know you may think I'm this fairy-type girl with her head in the clouds, constantly dreaming about her Prince Charming. I don't want love right now. I'm unsure if I will ever want it again after Jacob. But one thing I do know that I want is you. Whether that is in a relationship or just casually, I don't know. But all I do know is that I want to do this again and again and again."

Her smile was contagious. I knew better than to believe her, but my selfish tendencies didn't want to question it because I wanted this to happen again and again. So I let it pass.

We would deal with whatever disaster was ahead of us when the time came.

"In that case." I rolled us over, so I lay on my back, and she was straddling me. Her perky breasts filled my vision, and her nipples were hard already. "Ride me, sweetheart, so that I can say 'good morning' correctly."

And that she did. She rode me until she was sweaty and screaming my name while I drilled into her with every ounce of my power.

We were deep within the danger zone now. There was no turning back.

NATHANIEL

My days now consisted mainly of sex, work, and downtime with Amelia. The woman had me wrapped around her finger, and I could do nothing to stop her. I could deny her nothing. She had even talked me into a spa day last week so I could 'rejuvenate' my skin. I now knew the difference between salicylic acid and BHA serum.

The sex was terrific and electric. But in the moments after the sex had come and gone, as we just lay on the bed in silence, I felt closest to her in those silent moments.

There were layers to this girl that I had not even realized. She was funny but also incredibly intelligent. She had a passion for artistic things and found comfort in creating pieces and bringing them to life through her photography.

I could listen to her speak for hours and never grew tired of hearing her voice. It was the best part of my day. That and sending texts with her back and forth mainly consisted of memes, gifs, bad jokes, and pictures she took throughout the day on her phone.

Christmas was in two days, and my brother had again

tried to convince me to come home. I had declined. I was in no mood to play happy family with my father when I knew how he felt about me. Besides, I was going to spend my day with Amelia. Selena and Xander were heading out of town to go and visit their family. We were stuck with one another because Amelia had no family left, and I didn't want to see mine. I wasn't complaining.

But as I sat in my truck outside my apartment building, I sat there contemplating if I should make my usual trek up to her apartment, where we would have sex and watch one of the many shows she was trying to get me to love.

I had been sitting here thinking about the last call on my shift. A house had caught fire due to faulty heating. The old home was in flames within seconds. There had been three women trapped inside that house when we got there. A grandmother, a mother, and a little girl about seven years old: we managed to get the grandmother and child out, but the mother had been crushed by falling rubble.

I had to hold that little girl while she screamed for her mother. She had punched and kicked me, trying to run into the flames. She was so hysterical that we had to sedate her to transport her to the hospital. I held that little girl's hand until she woke up with tears.

Her name was Becca, and they had been baking her mom's birthday cake.

There were always days when you had hard calls, and today was one of those. We had been taught at the academy to avoid getting too attached to the various cases. And I had been pretty good at brushing off many of the horrors I had seen over the years, but this one hit home for me.

A knock came at my truck window, and I jumped in my seat. Amelia waved with a bright smile on her face and a red nose. When her eyes contacted mine, her smile dropped. She rounded the car and hopped into the passenger seat.

Her sweet scent filled my car, offering some semblance of comfort for me.

"What's wrong?" She grabbed my hand from across the console.

"Nothing. It's just work."

"Do you want to talk about it?"

"I don't want to dampen your mood. Let's go upstairs."

She frowned, looking from my face down to our hands. "I do love having sex with you, and I wouldn't mind having sex with you right now. However, I'd rather hear about why you look so down."

"Amelia." This was a heavy topic, and for someone as soft-hearted as Amelia, I didn't know if she could stand to hear about it.

"Hey, I asked because I want to know. Besides, a problem shared is a problem half solved."

Although I disagreed with her notion, I did understand it. But I was not used to sharing my feelings with someone. I had become so accustomed to carrying the entire load on my own. "I'm listening, but you must let me in, Nate."

"I lost someone today."

In my peripheral vision, I could see her body tense. "I'm sorry. Do you…do you want to talk about it, or do you want to leave it?"

I shrugged. "There isn't much to say. The mother got trapped under some rubble, and we couldn't free her. Her daughter had to watch their house go up in flames with her mother still in there."

She squeezed my hand, trying to offer me what little comfort she could give me. She sat in silence, waiting for me to let it all out.

"Her name is Becca. She's seven years old, and she was helping her mom make a birthday cake." The emotion parked right on my heart, crushing it ever so slightly. "They were just having a normal day, and then suddenly, her world flipped upside down. We could have saved her mom if we had arrived two minutes earlier. Maybe I could have saved her."

I knew that, logically, it was unlikely that we would have been able to do anything for Becca's mom. But that primary instinct to want to protect everyone always took over. I carried the guilt when I couldn't fulfill this God-like task. I had failed my mother once before and refused to fail anyone else. But when I couldn't protect those I loved, I was riddled with guilt and carried that weight.

"I know you love to be the hero, Nate. I know you take great pride in your work and ensuring everyone is okay. But you aren't God. You can't save everyone. You are simply one man, and you can't possibly think that you will save everyone in every disaster. It's not humanly possible."

These were all words that I had said to myself. But for some reason coming from her, they seemed to hold more weight. I was able to receive them with the kind of grace they required.

"You are a brilliant firefighter. I know that wherever you are on a call, those who need you are so blessed to have you there. You pour your all into your work, and I can see your love and passion. But don't place these extremely high standards on yourself. Allow yourself some grace."

She brought our intertwined fingers together and kissed every knuckle. When she was done, she pressed my hand into the center of her chest, where I could feel her heart's gentle, steady beating.

"I'm sorry about Becca and her mom. How is she doing now?"

"She will be in observation for the next three days and then leave with her grandmother."

"Is there anything that I can do for her? Maybe we can

set up a Go Fund Me for them to help pay off the funeral." There were moments when this girl wowed me, and this was one of them. "Why are you looking at me like that?"

"It's just that you don't even know her but are willing to do a fundraiser for her."

"You don't know her, but here you are, grieving her loss with her. Compassion and empathy are innate human attributes that we often need to tap into. I'm only doing what any compassionate and empathetic person would for a small needy child."

I stared at her, completely mind-blown.

Not only was she sexy with her toned runner legs and petite body. But the woman's heart was what shined through the most. I would even go as far as to say that it was the most beautiful part of her. It still astounded me how my brother could have ever let her go.

But that didn't matter. He was her past, and I was very much her present.

I kissed her lips softly, loving the feel of her on me. She tasted sweet, like strawberries and chocolate. When I pulled away, she had that bright megawatt smile that always managed to thaw out the ice from my heart.

"Tell me something real," she whispered.

This had become a kind of game we liked to play with one another. Every day one of us would ask this question, and the other would answer. It was mostly me because I wouldn't say I liked to open up to people. But I found that as the days passed, I was becoming more accustomed to revealing more and more of myself to Amelia. There was still one issue of the accident that I was yet to say anything about. My excuse was that the time wasn't right. But there would be no right time to tell her I was there the day she lost her mom because I had lost my mother too.

I resented her for it. Well, I had before now.

Those feelings of anger, guilt, and self-hatred had morphed into this poisonous rage I had attached to her. It had been unfair for me to do so. But in my head, it had been like a coping mechanism almost. I needed someone to hate. Since the woman who had driven her mother's car was dead, she was the only one I could attach my anger to.

Her hand cupped my cheek. "Hey, where did you go?"

I blinked away the past that threatened to spill over to this tender moment.

"Nowhere." I plastered a smile onto my face. "Hmm, let's see. Something real about myself...."

She sat beside me, silently waiting for me to speak. She played with my fingers absently as I tried to decide what side of me I would show here today. Up until this point, it had all been surface-level stuff. I never went too deep while she often revealed things that taught me more about her soul and the things that made it glow brighter.

I wanted her to know me. I wanted her to see me in ways no one had ever seen me.

"I have a journal," I confessed.

I had never told anyone about my journal. It was my best-kept secret.

"A journal?" She seemed shocked, which was expected, given how I carried myself. "Like one for workouts or an actual journal for your feelings."

"Yes, sweetheart." I tucked a stray strand of hair behind her ear. "A journal for feelings. I got it after my last tour of Syria. The therapist said that it could help with my PTSD."

The smile that had been playing on her lips faltered. Instant regret washed over her face. "I'm sorry I didn't mean to be insensitive."

"No, you weren't. Don't worry." I stared at our intertwined hands. "I thought it was stupid when he gave it to me. I wasn't a write-my-feelings-down kind of guy. But after

I tried it a few times when I was having trouble acclimating back to regular society, it helped. I could put my jumbled thoughts down and make sense of them. After a while, the damn thing became a lifeline for me. Now I write in it every day. Even if it's something stupid like I ate a doughnut today."

"You hate doughnuts." She made a face.

"Not all of them. I like the one from Sally's."

"Don't lie. You only ate half of your doughnut, then gave me the rest," she laughed.

"You were looking at it like a downcast puppy. I was performing a charitable act," I quipped back.

She slapped me playfully in the chest. "Charitable act? Hmph. And I was not looking like a downcast puppy."

"Yes, you were."

"No, I was not."

"Yes, you were."

And so began our debate on doughnuts and puppies, and just like that, she had turned my day around in less than an hour. She was becoming a staple in my day-to-day life. I feared that when the day to detach from her came, I wouldn't be able to do it.

21

_____

AMELIA

I was floating on cloud nine when I woke up. Nate was under the covers, and his mouth was on my wetness. He sucked and teased me to an orgasm. Then he took me from behind in the shower. We eventually got dressed and ready for our day.

We had built up a routine.

Sex. Getting him to love the same series as me. Talking. More sex. And then cuddle time.

Granted, cuddle time usually turned into more sex. We were insatiable for each other. After spending all of the Christmas holiday together and New Year's, you would think that hunger for each other would quell, but it didn't. If anything, I think it got more intense.

Now that we were well into the new year, I felt like a completely different woman. I was having mind-blowing sex with a man who was more complicated than a 10,000-piece jigsaw. There were many layers to the man, but he showed me glimpses of himself occasionally. Those sporadic yet memorable moments were the ones that I lived for.

I didn't notice Selena approach me outside the store. My

mind focused on Nate. It seemed that was all I could focus on nowadays.

I had been standing in the crisp winter air waiting for her. I was sure my nose and cheeks were red from the cold air.

I looked her up and down, taking in her red hair. "New look?"

She fluffed out her wavy red hair and winked. "I thought I would mix it up a bit. My life needed some dramatic flair in it."

So typical of Selena. She just moved with whatever mood she was in at the time. I wished I could do that too, but my inner control freak would never allow such to occur.

Where she daringly moved outside her box breaking past her comfort zone. I liked to stay within the parameter do predictability and safety.

"Okay, let's get this housewarming stuff." She clapped her hands together.

Today was her housewarming party. She had moved into a gorgeous townhouse that I loved. It suited her style so well; in typical Selena fashion, she wanted to throw a party for her 'house's birthday party.' Her words, not mine.

So here I was, being dragged out of my warm, comfy bed on a chilly Saturday morning. If this didn't show her that I loved her wholeheartedly, then I don't know what would. I was giving up precious sleep for this. And the way Nate and I had been going at it, I needed time to catch up on sleep.

"Okay, so we will need a variety of cheese, crackers, and other fancy stuff to make it look aesthetically pleasing to the eye. And then we are going to need some alcohol."

She grabbed her cart and led me down aisle after aisle as she picked things from the shelves.

My phone buzzed in my pocket, and when I went to

check it, I smiled instantly when I saw the name that flashed across the screen.

Nate: you replaced my shampoo.

I smiled.

Me: I didn't replace it. I accidentally put mine in your shower and forgot to return yours. Aww, do you smell like cherry blossoms and sweetness?

I would pay to see his reaction when he realized he was using my shampoo. He smelled wonderful, but I was tired of returning to my apartment to get my toiletries, so I stocked up on his.

Nate: this isn't funny. Xander is going to have a field day with this one. Thanks for that, sweetheart. I'm going to go around smelling like a freaking fruit punch.

Me: you are most welcome *kissy face emoji*besides who doesn't like to smell like fresh fruit. I think the scent will suit you well.

I could imagine his annoyed face right now.

Nate: How is grocery shopping?

Me: It's going fabulous except for the part where my best friend has turned into a bridezilla over this whole thing. I don't know what to do or say because I feel like the slightest thing could tick her off, and I'm not trying to end up on her wrong side.

Selena could be intimidating when she wanted to be. And I didn't want to face the hurricane storm she became when you wound up on her bad side.

Nate: It's her first home. It's a big moment for her. It's a given that she would want her housewarming to go well. Also, given that this is Selena, she is prone to over-dramatic tendencies.

This was true too.

Me: Are you coming tonight?

Nate: Of course. I want to see you in that red dress you tried on for me the other day. I can't have other men ogling what's mine.

A flutter moved within my chest. He always knew how to get me feeling flustered. Images of that night filled my mind. The way he had made me watch him undress me in the mirror. And after that, he then proceeded to pleasure me with his mouth as I sat at his dining table. I had been so shocked that it had managed to withstand the sheer force we had exerted on that thing.

"Earth to my best friend!" A packet of Doritos hit my head and took me from my thoughts. "Are you done having phone sex now?"

I blushed, "Phone sex? Who said I'm having phone sex?"

Selena stood beside the cart with Doritos in her hands and an annoyed expression.

"Your face. You're making that come and take me face you make when you're flirting with someone." Her eyes flicked back up to meet mine. "I know you've been having sex with Nate. Don't bother lying to me because that would only be an insult to our friendships and my intelligence."

Shame washed over me at the fact that I had been caught red-handed. I had planned to break the news to her differently.

"I'm sorry, Lena."

She waved me off. "I'm not mad at you, Lia. Besides, you suck at hiding your I've just had sex face, and you also have been extremely chipper lately. It wasn't hard to put two and two together. Also, I saw you sneak out of his apartment when I met you for coffee that day."

"What?" I had thought I was being so discreet.

"You suck at sneaking out, by the way. Everyone knows you need to do it under the cover of darkness. Rookie mistake," she teased me.

She analyzed my face for a few seconds.

"Brothers? Lia?"

I bit down on my lip. "I like him, Lena. It just feels exciting with him."

"Exciting or dangerous?"

"Both?"

She shook her head, looking at me how a parent would look at their child when they were worried for them. I knew what she was going to say before she even said it. That's how in tune we were with each other.

"Amelia," she began, and I prepared myself for what would come. "You just left one dusty Cane brother. Do you want to get involved with another? I don't want to ruin your fun or whatever you two are doing. But I can't sit back and watch you break again like you did with Jacob. Because Jacob is child's play compared to the damage Nate would do to you. I don't want to watch your heart shatter like that again."

"I'm not going to fall in love, Lena."

Her eyes softened, and she rounded the cart to where I stood. "Your heart is prone to love. You don't have room for detached things because they don't serve you in any way, shape, or form. And guarding your heart is like asking you to shut off pieces of yourself. The thing with you, Lia, is you love without caution. It doesn't matter to you how badly the person has wounded you or how deep they drove the knife. You would still find a way to love them."

Every point she made was like a slap to the face.

"I don't want to watch you break into a million pieces again after you picked every last shard and put it in its place." Her voice came out rougher, her words laden with emotions that I was surprised were coming out. Selena was more of the "don't show any emotion" person. She wasn't the mushy gushy person that bears her heart and soul. "You are deserving of a kind and healing love. I won't say I support your decision to try things with him, but I want you to know that I'm behind you, and regardless of the outcome, I will always be here."

She pulled me into a hug.

I wanted to tell her that her fears were all vain and that I was terrific. I tried telling her I wouldn't fall in love with Nathaniel Cane. But the only problem was that I was already falling for him, and it was only a matter of time before my back hit the ground.

22

AMELIA

The house party was in full swing. Everyone was milling about Selena's new house, talking amongst each other.

The house was beautiful and everything you would expect from Selena Montgomery.

Lavish. Chic. Expensive looking.

She had purchased a beautiful townhouse in the middle of the city. It was a nice, quiet neighborhood, unlike my area. Not to say my neighborhood was terrible, but it was more of a downtown vibe than uptown.

Hardwood floors and vaulted ceilings. Black marble kitchen and open plan living and dining room. The house was modern yet very tasteful. And the neutral color scheme Selena had chosen throughout the house only added to the expensive feel of the home. She even had a little backyard. It wasn't massive but good enough to have a small garden with the flowers she loved to plant.

I knew I was far from affording something like this, but I hoped to move into something like this once my photography took off like I wanted it to.

All these dreams I had harbored for years had been pushed to the back burner for years because of Jacob. I had made him the center of my universe for so long, and now I was finally living for me. And it felt so good.

When I moved to Chicago, the last thing I had expected was to get entangled with his brother. But here I was in whatever Nate and I were. I knew I wasn't far from loving the man, which scared me. I couldn't risk it, either. I had already allowed one Cane brother to ruin me. But Nate set something inside of me alight.

But the fire was also warm before it burned you, and I knew that would be Nate for me at some point, but I didn't want to think about it. I didn't want to think about the possibility of an end for us.

"What are you doing here looking all sexy and alone?" His hot breath fanned the nape of my neck, causing the hairs on my back to stand up. I whirled around on my heels to stare at him.

My goodness, this man was pure perfection.

The dress code had been dressy casual, and the man had delivered on that. He wore tailored pants, a clean white button-down, and two undone top buttons. This man seemed to be from another world. That was the only way I could describe what I was seeing. And he smelled like temptation and sin all wrapped up into one.

"Checking me out, Lia?" His husky voice tickled the little button in my core that automatically switched on when he was around. His eyes ravaged my body in a heated stare. I could feel his touch simply from how his eyes focused on my skin. "I like the dress."

The tips of my lips tilted upward. "You did say I should wear it."

The red dress had been a casual buy, and I had forgotten I had it until Selena told me she wanted to do a housewarming. It was an off-the-shoulder cocktail dress that hugged my body like a second skin. There was a slit that ran down the side of the dress, adding to that va va voom factor.

"I did, but now I have to pull myself back from punching all the idiots eyeing you like their last meal." His eyes darkened, the electricity between us shooting out at all angles. "I didn't envision myself spending the night in a jail cell for aggravated assault."

The air left my lips in a breathless gasp. "Oh really?"

He stepped in closer, leaning close to my ear so he could whisper. Immediately I was invaded by his scent. Leather, pine, and spice. It was intoxicating, and I could simply get drunk off of this alone. His hand found its place on my hip. "You drive me crazy, Amelia."

The shiver that went down my spine reminded me of just how much of an effect this man had on me. He could turn my body on with one look, one touch, one gaze.

People surrounded us, but they all faded into the distance, and all I could see was him.

I looked back into his eyes. "Do you want to know something, Mr. Cane?"

"Tell me, Lia." Oh, how he said my name was like sweet honey to my ears.

I stepped beside him, my heels making it so I could reach his ear without straining too much. I leaned close to mimic what he had just done to me a few seconds ago.

"I'm not wearing any underwear." When I pulled away, I was satisfied with the tortured and hungry expression in his eyes. "Do with that information what you will. As for me, I need to go and help my friend hand out little tiny hotdogs."

I scurried away with a triumphant smile on my face.

I walked over to Selena, who was talking to one of her coworkers. When she saw me approach, she excused herself and met me halfway. She looked dazzling in a cream cocktail dress that hugged her body in all the right places, causing a stir among the men in this room. I didn't know any of these people, but seeing Selena so at ease and happy with them made me like them.

Selena smiled at me, her eyes moving in the direction I had come from. It didn't take her long to connect my smile and Nate's heated gaze. "No sex in my room, but you can take the guest room if you want."

I blushed. "That's okay. I think you should have the honor of christening your house first."

"Oh, I did," she winked while sipping her flute. "Three times last night and once this morning."

"Oh, my gosh!" I poked her side. "Who? Don't tell me it was Xander?"

"Wouldn't you like to know?"

"Umm, yes. That's why I'm asking." My eyes moved to Xander, who had just turned the corner to walk into the living room. He dressed similarly to Nate but didn't hold the same wow factor that Nate did for me. "Do you like him, Lena?"

She lifted her shoulder in a slight shrug. "Like is such a strong word. Why don't we just say that I enjoy his company."

Selena was one of those people who hated being vulnerable or talking about her feelings. She preferred not to have emotions attached to anything. That included men most of all. She had always been that way, and I had no idea why.

"I swear his eyes move everywhere you are. I'm trying to decide if it's creepy or weird."

Standing in the corner of the room, looking so delicious, was Nate and Xander beside him. They were both looking in our direction, and Xander looked at my best friend like he wanted to devour her. But there was also something else in his eyes. Something a little more, and I was unsure if Selena had caught on to it.

He liked her. I had seen the eyes of a man falling, and those were the eyes he was giving her.

"Oh look, Nate's coming over here." She nudged me. "I bet you ten bucks he will take you home right now."

Just as she said, Nate walked over to me. His eyes held mine the entire time. I even had to will my heart rate down. It felt like it wanted to jump right out of my chest.

"I think this is my cue to exit the vicinity." She slid away just as Nate came to a grinding halt. "Good luck."

Nate snaked his arm around my waist and pulled me flush against him. His hard chiseled chest was warm beneath my palms, and I could feel his heart's slow and steady beating.

At least one of us was calm.

"Let's get out of here."

"So soon?"

He huffed, the tip of his lips tilting upward ever so slightly. He leaned in, his lips brushing my scorching skin. "You have ten minutes to say your goodbyes, and I'm taking you home. You take any more time than that, Amelia, and I will have to throw you over my shoulder and slap that perky little ass of yours."

My body buzzed with excitement. Part of me wanted to take the extra time and force him to do something. As weird as that sounded, I wanted him to handle me like a flour sack.

His lips pressed against my skin, drawing me out of my thoughts. "Come now, baby. Let me take you home."

"Okay." my spine shivered as I tried to keep myself from entirely losing it.

When he pulled away, his eyes were a darker shade of green. The hunger in his eyes was potent, but I could see him holding himself back. This man wanted me, and if the moistness in the middle of my legs was saying anything, I wanted him to.

"Let's go home," he encouraged.

I nodded wordlessly.

"Good girl. Now say goodbye to your friend and meet me outside."

He took a few steps back, making me miss his warmth over me again. "Ten minutes starts now, Amelia."

I didn't know what awaited me with this man, but I was excited to find out.

23

AMELIA

Nate cut the engine off in the basement parking of the building. He had his hand on my knee the entire way home, finger-stroking my soft skin. The heat that had pulled into my core, making my lower half throb was unlike anything I had ever experienced.

I had been taken and pleasured by this man like there was no tomorrow. One would think that the hunger would have died down after so many nights together, but it only intensified. The man was like ecstasy. He was like my own personal brand of heroine.

Addictive. Intense. All consuming.

I turned to find this man looking at me with darkened eyes. Only one thing was swimming in his eyes: desire. I was sure that my eyes mirrored his. I was hungry for him in ways I had never been for someone in my entire life.

The tension in the air was thick. There was the subtle buzz of electricity. The atmosphere was supercharged.

"Spread them, Lia." His command was low but clear.

"What?" My voice didn't even sound like my own.

"Spread. Your. Legs."

I looked out the window at the semi-full parking bay. It was just empty cars and no people, and his truck's windows were moderately tinted. But this seemed….risky.

"But…"

He leaned over the console, my body already shivering with the anticipation of his touch. "Spread."

I didn't need to be told twice. I opened my legs for the man. His hands moved from the slit of my dress and slowly crept in on the inside of my thigh.

His mouth moved toward my neck, his lips brushing against mine, causing me to shiver.

The man had barely touched me, and I already wanted to burst. My legs spread even further when I felt the gentle brush of his fingertips.

His forefinger swiped at my swollen lips, catching some of the slickness. I had to bite my lips to keep the moan from escaping.

"So wet for me." As he spoke, his lips brushed against my skin, causing my pussy to throb. "Were you wet the entire time, Amelia? Hmm?"

He dipped not one but two fingers into my entrance, and I all but melted into the seat.

I spread my legs as wide as they could go. His fingers teased me up and down like never before. My back arched into the seat's leather.

"So greedy for me, baby." His hot breath fanned my skin.

"Here or my bed." That was all he said. The roughness in his voice tickled at something inside of me.

"What?"

He brushed a stray strand of hair that had left its place. My eyes followed the movement of his hand, my entire heart practically in my mouth.

"Can I ravage you here or in my bed?"

The directness in his tone set my entire body on fire. "Your bed."

We had been having sex at mine all the time, and now I wanted to see his place. I wanted him to touch me in his sanctuary. I wanted him to kiss me under his showerhead. I wanted to christen every inch of that apartment as we had mine.

He slipped his fingers out of me. Then he hopped out of the car and rounded it until he came to my door. He ripped it open and threw me over his shoulder like a flour sack. I let out a few shrieks, to which he answered with a slap on my ass.

"Someone is feeling frisky," I laughed like a little schoolgirl.

"You think you're funny, Amelia?" He slapped my ass again. "I've got something for that smart mouth of yours."

We both laughed.

The butterflies that filled my stomach were intense, and the anticipation that flooded my body only added to the lust-filled frenzy.

We walked into his apartment after one elevator ride and a few strides. I had no chance to look over the area because the lights were all out, and he headed straight for his room.

The man had a one-track mind.

He placed me on the bed, my body bouncing off the mattress. I didn't have time to fully recover because I was being hoisted back onto my feet the next thing I knew.

We stripped each other down, layer by layer, until we were left bare in front of each other.

My hands moved up and down his chiseled body. My hands trace every curve and crevasse on this beautiful master-piece. He could give David a run for his money.

I reached in between us, grabbing onto his hardened

length. He let out a low hiss near my ear, causing the hairs on my neck to stand up.

I pumped his hard cock in my hand, his hand's grip tightly on my hips. I kissed his shoulder, pushing up onto my toes to place my mouth right by his ear.

"How did you say you would make me shut up again?"

He pulled back so quickly that I had no time to register his movements fully. He grabbed my chin and tilted my head so I could stare into his fiery eyes.

"Baby…"

"I want to," I whispered back. "I want to take all of you into my mouth, please."

I never thought I would ever be begging a man to let me blow him, but here I was. I wanted to see him come undone at the mercy of my mouth. I tried to tease and push him over the edge as he did with me countless times.

He kissed me intensely, searing me with his burn. I gently pushed us back until the back of his legs hit the bed and made him lie down. He moved all the way up so his head lay on the headrest. He stroked his length with his eyes trained on me.

"I'm waiting, love."

He didn't need to say anymore. I crawled on top of him and took his tip into my mouth. I teased him a little, earning the moans and hisses I wanted. Then I took him all in right down to the very back of my throat.

This man was big and taking him all in was hard for me without gagging a little. But the sound only made his cock twitch.

He liked it.

He placed his hand on my head, guiding me as my head bobbed up and down, sucking him as if my life depended on it. My throbbing only increased just from hearing him moan beneath me. It was begging to be touched and teased like I was teasing him.

As if he had read my mind, Nate reached behind and plunged three fingers into me, filling me to the max. I tried to keep the same rhythm, but it was hard to concentrate when he moved in and out of me, tickling my walls ever so slightly.

He thrust his hips upward and I gagged.

He let out a low growl and his cock popped out of my mouth.

I was about to protest to have him in my mouth again, but my words were stolen right from my lips when he removed his fingers and grabbed me by my hips. He set me down just before his length, his hands gripping my hips.

"Put it in," he pecked my lips. "Keep your eyes on me."

I lifted, and he held his length straight for me. He angled it by my entrance, and I slowly lowered myself onto him.

I kept my eyes locked on his. The electricity that moved between us was like magic and drugs.

Inch by inch, he filled me.

Our moans melded together in unison, a perfect harmony of euphoria and raw lust.

"Ride my dick, baby," he groaned, holding me down. "I want to see you from down here."

And ride his dick I did.

I lifted before slamming myself down and feeling him in every pore. I moved up and down, ensuring I did not waste a single inch of his big cock.

"Fuck me," I whispered.

"You like me in you, don't you?" He drew me down toward him, his lips capturing mine. He wound his arms around me, held me flush against him, and pounded into me with no mercy.

"Ah," I screamed into the room. "Yes…oh my, yes."

Sweat beaded his forehead, so he worked me closer and closer to the edge.

In one swift motion, he flipped us over so I lay at the bottom, and he lay between my legs. He continued his fast pounding while I continued meeting him thrust for thrust.

"Baby…" he groaned, taking my nipple into his mouth, "fuck, you feel like a dream."

His words only pushed me further toward the cliff edge.

"You take me so well." He traced his tongue along my puckered nipples. "Every. Last. Inch."

"Nate, I'm going to…" I was barely hanging on at this point. I was so close to the edge, so close to finding my release, but I wanted to wait for him.

"I'm right there with you, baby." He brushed my hair away from my face, his eyes locking with mine.

I don't know what it was, but something shifted. I couldn't quite put my finger on it, but something moved between us that felt like…I didn't know if I could even say the word.

I closed my eyes as the beginning tingles spread from my core. His hand grabbed my chin, forcing me to open my eyes.

"Eyes open. On me."

He moved in and out of me until we finally came undone.

Our orgasms ripped through us violently as the euphoric feeling overtook us. The high lasted much longer than before, and this clouded haze of pure and utter bliss settled over us.

This was different. This wasn't just us having sex for the sake of release. This was…more. This was sensual. This was passion. This was…making love.

I had waited for the panic to settle, but that feeling never came. All I felt was calm and peace.

When we settled, he pulled out of me, lying beside me.

He pulled me into his chest, his mouth kissing my forehead gently.

I closed my eyes, just relishing the feeling of having him this close to me. I never wanted this to end, but in the back of my mind, I knew that one day we would have to come to an end. Only I didn't know if I could survive our conclusion.

I was spent. My body was satisfied like it had never been before. There was just something about the way this man handled me that left me...floating. We had had sex many times before, but this time felt so different. At first, it had been stiff and dirty and raw, but then somewhere in between, when we were facing each other, it turned into more than just fucking. We made love in its purest form. I had waited for the terror to overtake me and the alarm bells to ring in my head, but I felt none of that. I was so at peace at the thought of making love to this man.

I remembered every touch, every kiss, and every gaze. I wanted to commit it all to memory because I didn't know when next I would experience him like this.

The scary thing was that even with Jacob, it had never been like this, and I had known Jacob for years.

The moon streamed in from the window casting this blue hue over our skin.

"Sleep." He pulled me into him, his tiredness coating his voice. "I can hear your brain thinking."

"You sleep." I placed my hand on top of his on my bare stomach. His legs were draped over mine securely. I was going nowhere.

"I'm trying, but I can hear your brain thinking." He yawned a low chuckle.

"Why did you hate me before?" I don't know why I was

bringing this up now, seeing we were trying to sleep after mind-blowing sex. But the question had plagued me and he had never thoroughly answered it.

"What do you mean?" He asked.

I licked my lips, bracing myself for what I would say to this man. My eyes looked out to the Chicago skyline. The various sky-rise buildings and streetlights illuminate downtown Chicago. You didn't get this in Braven, that was for sure.

"When I was with Jacob. You hated me, or at least I thought you did. You never said it in so many words, but your actions spoke volumes." He hummed in answer, and I was too scared to look back to see his face. "So why?"

"I never hated you…" he said in a sleepy voice fighting back another yawn. "I hated myself for what I did to you and…"

I waited, with bated breath, "…and?"

"My mom."

That didn't make any sense. What had he done to me and his mother that made him hate himself? Nate's mom passed away when I was about six years old. I didn't even know Jacob back then. I met him a year later when I transferred schools after my accident.

I turned in his arms to look into his eyes, but my mouth slammed shut when I saw his eyes closed and felt his heavy and low breathing.

He was asleep. He was utterly knocked out.

I couldn't help but smile at how his long lashes kissed his cheekbones, and his brown hair flopped over his forehead.

I wanted to know what he meant by his comment, but I also knew he would likely not remember it come morning. So, like most things when it came to him, I pushed it down and hoped it didn't bubble back up after some time.

24

AMELIA

I loved many things in this world, but waking up next to Nate had to be one of my favorites. This time he had taken me into his apartment.

All the other times we had had sex, he always came over to mine. I knew how he was about his space, so the fact that he took that step with me was huge.

Last night he had been so perfect in every way.

Now, I stood in the crisp morning air taking pictures of Amber, my new client, for her maternity shoot. She was glowing from the life she had created inside her. We decided to come to the park to get some nature shots without having to leave the city for it.

I had to be up at the crack of dawn to get the lighting I needed. And it had been even more difficult to leave because the man who had his arms around me was far too comfortable.

"So stunning, Amber," I beamed at her.

She smiled back, rubbing her belly. "Thank you, Amelia."

Her husband stood off the side, looking at his wife with

awe. Mike was a saint, to the least. He had been doting on her the entire time.

"I think we got it." I looked down at the small screen of my camera and saw the shots I had taken so far. She looked stunning.

She wore a long white maternity dress that flowed to the floor. With the gentle breeze that had been picking up here and there, the skirt had lifted just the slightest bit, giving it this ethereal look. Her blonde hair even had a flower crown in it.

"You're smiling," she gushed, waddling over to me. "Are they good?"

"You are stunning, Amber." I showed her the camera and waited for her reaction.

Her blue eyes brightened, and her smile widened. "Oh, my goodness. You made me so pretty. I love them."

"No," I said. "That's all you."

Her husband came up behind her and kissed her temple warmly before placing an oversized coat over her petite frame. "She truly is a stunner."

His eyes watched her with so much love swimming in them. The moment felt so intimate that I felt like I was intruding on something special between the two.

"I will have these in for you in three days."

Tears brimmed the mommy-to-be's eyes. "Of course. And I'm so sorry for being like this. I'm just so…hormonal."

"You're good."

"Aww baby," her husband pulled her toward his chest. He then smiled at me. "Thank you, Amelia. We look forward to seeing the pictures."

"Of course," I said my goodbyes and went to where I had left my bag by the bench.

I bent over to organize my bag when I felt someone looming over me. I snapped back up and whirled around to find Nate standing with two coffees in one hand and a small bag in the other.

"You left early," he said as he held the small tray of two coffees out of me. "Yours is the one on the right."

I arched my brow asking, "Do you even know my order?"

"Caramel and hazelnut latte with oat milk and three drops of stevia."

I blinked, my mouth gaping wide. "How…how do you know that?"

"Whenever I came over, you always had a cup of coffee in hand, or you were among some."

I thought back to the times he had shown up, and I was deep in editing mode. He would wait patiently and sit while I did my work. I had made both coffees several times but had not told him what I put in my coffee. He liked his coffee one way—black.

I know. So plain and boring, but it suited him. I couldn't imagine him drinking something sweet like my caramel latte. The black coffee embodied him perfectly—strong, dark, and unforgivingly one taste.

"And you paid attention to all of that?" I took the cup slowly from the tray, still eyeing him like I was looking at some extraterrestrial creature. I took a small sip, not believing he had gotten my order right.

But as soon as the hot liquid hit my tongue, I was in shock.

"Oh, wow! You got it right."

"Of course I did." The tips of his lips slowly tilted upward just the slightest bit. "Come on. You're hungry, and I have never been in this park."

"What? You've lived here for years and never been to Aubrey Park. It's ten minutes from our building."

"Does it look like I ever explored parks?"

"I mean, you have this tortured artist thing going on." I

145

gestured to his entire body. "You also scowl a lot. Like you barely smile."

He arched an eyebrow. "I smile."

"Yeah, at me." It felt good that he did. "But even to Selena. She said hi the other day when we saw you coming into the building, and you scowled. You didn't even say, 'Hi.' You just grunted—like an ape."

"An ape? Is this any way to speak to the man who came and brought you sustenance?"

I tilted my head to the side, taking him in for a little while. The way the sun was hitting his face just right caused this golden glow to fall on his face. He was majestic—there was no other way to explain it. The green of his eyes partially faded, giving way to some blue, taking on a more hazel tint.

"Come on, grumpy." I grabbed my bag and swung it over my shoulder.

"I can get that for you."

I shook my head. "This is where my baby is. No one touches it except for me."

He held his hands up and surrendered. "My apologies."

"Okay, come on. Let's walk."

We fell into step with each other walking through the park as if we did it daily.

NATHANIEL

There were few things in this life that I could tolerate. Amelia just happened to be one of those things. It was strange to me how this woman had just bulldozed her way into my life, and I had allowed her.

I had fought her. Oh, how I had tried pushing her back. But she was persistent. There was this thing when it came to Amelia. She had a way of burrowing herself into your life and making it feel like she belonged there. It was like a takeover but in the most gentle way possible.

Fuck. I sounded like Xander.

I was far from a lover boy—the exact opposite. I had seen too much, and my heart was so scared that I didn't even know if it still functioned correctly.

But walking with her like this in the park felt so…easy. It felt natural.

"Tell me something real about you," she said as she bit into her doughnut with the biggest smile. The woman was so easy to please it was wild.

"What do you mean?"

"Something real," she said, nearly choking on her bite as

she tried to speak. "Sorry, but these are so good. Oh, it's like heaven."

She bit into it again, but this time moaning and enjoying the flavors that danced in her mouth. The sound alone brought flashbacks of last night. Her screams of pleasure were firmly engraved in my mind now. I got hard just thinking about it.

"Nate?"

"Sorry, what?"

"I asked for you to tell me something real about yourself." She blinked. "Like something real and raw about you."

Real and raw? That was a big ask for a man like me. I had many scars from my time in Syria and the accident. But many others were hidden. Wounds that had never quite healed. Wounds that she had a hand in creating—or at least I thought she did.

"I held my best friend's hand when we got blasted in Hama, Syria. And I watched the life fade from his eyes." I hated reliving this memory. This happened six years ago on my first tour. Six years and the wounds still had not healed, much like the ones from the night of the accident. "His name was Andre. The guy always wound up in trouble one way or another. He loved the thrill of it—the danger that is. He said that he loved teetering on the edge of life and death. It's one of the major reasons he signed up for the Marines in the first place."

"He sounds fun."

"He was. The guy always had a smile on his face. It was like nothing fazed him. He never let the job steal his light."

I thought back to Andre and all the moments that we shared. He had been more than just my buddy in the service. He was my brother. We had built a bond and seen each other through much hardship. Being out there in the line of fire changed a man. It wore on your soul, but somehow Andre managed to keep me grounded. He managed to hold me down even when I felt like spiraling.

"It was meant to be just one of those routine trips by escorting civilians, but then we got hit by a suicide bomber. The shrapnel lodged itself in his heart." My throat tightened just thinking about that day. "I had seen many people fall in the line of duty. I had seen many people lose limbs. But it never hit me quite as hard as it did that day. This wasn't just some colleague ....this was my...my brother."

I had never told anyone this story aside from Xander. It was a dark mark in my past that I wouldn't say I like to revisit.

"He had knocked me to the ground to take the shot at the bomber, but it was too late. The bomb went off, and he put his body on top of mine when he heard the explosion." My voice tightened at the end of my sentence. Reliving these memories was like picking at a scab and realizing the wound was still fresh underneath. "We were too far out from the base for them to get there on time, so I just sat beside him and held his hand while he took his last breath on this earth."

I remembered it all so clearly in my mind. I watched the light drain from his eyes as his chest rose for the last time.

His last words to me were, 'Stop existing and start living.'

He knew of the accident, and he knew of my strained relationship with my brother and father. But above all of that, he knew of Amelia. He knew what she represented to me or at least what she had previously meant to me.

He was the one person on this earth who knew me through and through. I hadn't even told Xander about Amelia and our connection with the accident, and I don't think I ever would. The wounds with Amelia were just far too deep.

A small hand fit into mine, bringing my stride to a

grinding halt. I looked at Amelia, her delicate features and eyes almost liquefied with emotion.

"I'm sorry for your loss." Her voice was so soft it could have been a whisper. "And I'm sorry you've had to carry those scars for so long."

I was taken aback by how sincere she sounded. Her tone had no forced empathy—just complete and utter sincerity.

She let out a short breath, her shoulders rising and falling quickly. "I didn't watch her die, but I was involved in an accident with my mom, as you already know. She had been working the night shift then, and I had come down with something. We had been on our way to the hospital when she hydroplaned and lost control of the car."

My heart stopped in my chest.

This was the one topic that I didn't want to visit with her, but I didn't stop her. She had allowed me to show my demons. Now she wanted to show me hers.

"I blamed myself." A bitter laugh escaped her lips. "I always thought that maybe if I didn't get sick, then maybe, just maybe, she would be alive."

"Amelia—"

"I know, I know." She started walking us back down the path. "It was simply an accident, and it could have happened to anyone, but I just…I wish it hadn't been us. But isn't that bad, however? Because if it weren't us, it would have been some other poor family. I wouldn't hand the card I was dealt that day to anyone else."

The same card we had been dealt. But she didn't know that. She didn't know that on that very day she lost her mother, I lost mine too. She didn't think I had been in her room at the hospital. I had seen her hooked up to all those machines and wished her soul would be taken instead of my mother's. She didn't know I had connected her to the worst moment of my life for years. There had been resentment and, dare I even say, hatred. But as the years passed and I watched her with my brother, I just knew that someone so filled with light could not be capable of hurting a soul. That's when I shifted the blame to myself.

"It's not bad. You wanted your mom around, which doesn't make you bad. It makes you human."

The slight pout and quiver of her lip were enough to be my undoing. "Maybe. But after she died, I don't know. I just stopped living and just existed. My entire life had felt like it was on autopilot until—" she cut herself off before continuing. Her eyes stared into space. The sadness was evident on her face, but there was a twinkle in her eye that I had never seen before.

"Until…?" I pressed her.

"Until I moved here and began figuring out what I wanted out of this life and who I wanted to be."

"And have you figured out what you want out of life?" I watched her profile, trying to gauge her reaction. Amelia wore her feelings on her face. There was no mistaking her feelings because she was like an open book.

She turned to look up at me. The sadness—although reduced—was still present, but a small smile sparked her eyes. "Yeah. I think so."

I had always been clear about what I wanted out of life. I knew what I wanted when I left the Marines and set my feet back on American soil. But now, with her in my life, she was throwing everything out of whack, and I was beginning to want things I was sure I could not sustain.

My head was fucked. One thing I did know for sure was that I needed to tell this woman truth.

26

NATHANIEL

Coming off my Wednesday shift, I received zero texts from Amelia. This was unlike her. After our date in the park, something shifted for me.

I hadn't planned on telling her about Andre. The words had just slipped from my mouth. There were very few people in this world who knew about Hama. Xander had been one of them. Now, so was Amelia.

Andre was a soft spot for me and a topic I always avoided. Xander knew to avoid bringing it up.

I had waited for the regret to sink in after I had told Amelia about it, but it never came. And that was what scared me. She was close, a little too close for comfort. She was light and energetic and all things beautiful. And I was dark scars and hatred. But now, the hatred was not toward her. Hatred was the opposite of what I felt for her. I had not known that to be possible. Not with anyone else.

It was all meant to be physical. That was what I knew I could give her. That was what I had been sure I was capable of. But this thought circled in my head for the last few days, making me question whether there was more that I was capable of.

'Stop existing and start living.' Those had been the words of my best friend. His last words to me were to start seeing the light.

I rechecked my phone like a lovesick teenager to see if she had texted me, and there was nothing.

I didn't worry easily. My line of work made me relaxed and always composed. But the longer she kept quiet, the more irrational my thoughts became. I had seen people die from stupid things and unintentional acts.

What if she slipped and hit her head in the shower? What if carbon monoxide was leaking into her studio? What if she accidentally drank a poison, confusing it for a drink?

All these crazy theories filtered into my head and only made my panic increase instead of subsiding.

Deciding to jump the gun, I dialed her number as I exited my truck and headed upstairs to my apartment. The phone rang with no answer from the other side. I was getting increasingly worried. I dialed again, but just like before, there was no answer from the other side.

Where had she disappeared to?

I got into the elevator and pressed the floor number. But as I went up, my mind was only filled with Amelia and what was happening with her today. Had I pissed her off? I had a knack for doing that without even trying most days.

The doors to the elevator dinged open, but instead of turning left, I headed right toward this woman's door. Was I being a little too persistent? Maybe. But what if her apartment did have a carbon monoxide leak? She could be suffocating, and I would have done nothing to help her.

I came to her door, redialing her number. I banged on the door simultaneously, hoping that she would hear it. But no such luck on her answering either.

"Amelia?" I called out to her. "Amelia? Are you okay?"

I knocked on the door harder and frantically, hoping she could hear me.

"Amelia, if you don't open up, I will be forced to break this door down," I said after a loud silence. "Amelia!"

It was safe to say I was nervous. She was never like this, and I didn't have Selena's number to check on her. I knew Xander would have it, but I was already here.

I took a few steps back, ready to break the door down, but then the knob twisted. It slowly creaked open. Behind it stood a very pale-looking Amelia with a blanket over her body.

"Amelia?"

Her eyes had dark circles under them, and her face was as white as a ghost. I could see the sweat droplets gathering on her forehead.

"Nate?" Her voice was so weak, her body leaning against the door frame.

I rushed to her side. As soon as my hands touched her skin, I felt the heat. "Jesus, you're burning up."

She nodded weakly, her head coming to rest on the door frame. "I've been sick all day. It started with a sore throat, and now I—woah. I feel dizzy."

She tried to move off the frame and head back inside, but I stopped her and scooped her into my arms. She didn't even protest. Her body just instinctively curled into mine. Her petite frame wracked against me.

"Oh no, Amelia." I carried her inside and walked us to her bed.

I could see from the state of her studio that she had been in bed all day. Her sheets were rumpled, and the table had uneaten takeout.

I gently placed her on the bed. "Have you seen a doctor?"

She shook her head. "It's just a bug. I need to sleep it off."

"And how long have you been sleeping it off?"

She blinked up at me, her eyes barely able to stay open. "What day is it today?"

"Wednesday." I brushed the strands of her hair away from her face. She didn't look good at all.

"I got sick on Monday."

"You texted me and said you were fine on Monday."

"And I was." Another shiver wracked her body. "It just went downhill yesterday."

"You should have called me." I left and went to her bathroom, where she kept a medicine cabinet. "What have you taken so far?"

"Nothing," she croaked out.

I stuck my head out of the bathroom. "Are you serious?"

She blinked from her bed. Her mouth made an oh shape. "Yes?"

"You are going to be the death of me one of these days, Amelia." I went back to the bathroom and got the necessary medication.

I sat back on the bed and gave her the correct dosages to help her fever and pain. I grabbed the cup on her bedside table and helped her sit up. I placed her back against my chest and drew the water to her lips.

"Take the meds, Lia."

She did as she was told and took the meds, then took the water when I tipped the glass into her mouth. After she was done, she leaned against me, her back melting into my front. She closed her eyes, her hands taking mine and placing them on her stomach.

"You're here." It was more of a question rather than a statement.

"I wanted to check on you. You weren't answering your phone."

I looked down to see her lips tilting upward slightly. "So you were worried about me then? Awww, does the brooding man have a soft spot for me."

More than you would ever know. But there was no way I would say that, so I resorted to something a little more casual.

"Shut up."

"It's okay," she yawned. "I know you care."

Her fingers interlaced with mine. Then she tilted her head up. Her eyes were much duller than usual, but that little Amelia sparkle was there.

"How was work?" She smiled up at me. "Did you just get off?"

I brushed her cheek, loving the soft feel of her skin under my thumb. "I did. You should sleep."

"But I want to talk to you instead."

"I'll be here when you wake up."

"Promise?"

I nodded. "I promise."

"Okay." She turned back, resting the back of her head on my chest. Within minutes her breathing regulated, and she fell asleep in my arms. Her hands were still clutching onto mine, and her body was warm, but at least the medication would have time to work.

I lay with her for some time before I finally decided it was best for me to lay her down.

The wiser thing would have been to leave her to rest and check on her later, but I couldn't bring myself to leave her like that. So I decided to stay and play Nurse Nate.

I cleaned her studio and even ordered some soup for her. I put away the dishes she had cleaned the night before and organized her desk.

While putting away one of her books, I spotted a picture on her desk. It was a Polaroid of me lying on her couch, knocked out cold. I remembered when this day was. She had been editing the entire day. I had come over for a quick little session, but I had been so tired from the day before that I just passed out cold. When I woke up again, the sun had fallen, and it was dinner time. She had made me some chicken soup and had forced me to watch Marvel movies.

She had said they were her favorite but hated them, from what I could tell. She had only done it because she knew I liked them.

That was the thing about Lia. She always thought of everyone else's needs before her own. She was the embodiment of selflessness, which was even more apparent to me after today. She had the kindest and most gentle heart. And I had been an asshole.

I flipped the Polaroid around and saw her little inscription at the back.

'My brooding sunshine'

I smiled.

Call it an aha moment, or call it whatever you want to. But in that second, that's when it all fully clicked. I couldn't deny it now, even if I wanted to.

I loved her.

I was in love with my brother's ex-girlfriend and that scared the shit out of me.

27

AMELIA

I had been sick for the past two weeks. After that night, when Nate had come to nurse me back to health, I had been fine. But then I started feeling sick all over again. I had been unable to keep anything down for the past three days. Selena had joked that maybe I was with a child. Then when I thought back on it, I realized that I was three days late on my period.

Being on the pill made me very regular in my cycle. So it was odd that I was suddenly late.

But there was no way because I took the pill every day at the same time. I was very strict with myself, especially now that I was active. I needed to ensure that there were no slip-ups.

But that was a little late because I was reading the back of a pregnancy box.

"You just got to pee in it," Selena called on the other side of the door. "Do it in the cup and then dip it in."

"That sounds gross." My hands were quite literally shaking.

"Bitch, pee in the damn cup." She yelled from the other side.

I had been here staring at the box like it would eat me. I was at a loss for words, if I was being honest. I was also terrified. If I was pregnant, what would that mean for me and Nate? I loved the guy. We had established that, but we weren't in a relationship. The man was terrified of commitment, and a baby superseded loyalty. That was a lifetime connection.

Would he even want to be involved with the baby?

I closed my eyes and took a few calming breaths, trying to prepare myself for what I was about to do.

I got to work, took the cup I had been given, and peed in it. I then dipped the test inside and placed it under the box. When I was done, I opened the door for my best friend to come in.

"How long?" She tried to look under the box, but I grabbed her hand.

"Ten minutes. Then I should have a result." Even my focus was trembling, but Selena just held my hand. She reassured me that regardless of what would show on the screen, we would tackle it one step at a time.

"Have you told Nate you're taking a test?"

I shook my head. "Why worry him? The test could come back negative. Besides, he's at work and has another 12 hours on his shift. He doesn't need this right now."

That and I was also scared to tell him. The emotions with him were genuine, and now this? It was wild.

The timer I had set on my phone went off.

"Oh my gosh," I whimpered, clutching my best friend's hand. "I'm scared."

Selena squeezed my hand. "I'm right here with you."

I felt like I was going to be sick.

"Hey!" she grabbed my chin and forced me to look at her. "Whatever it says, I got you, okay?"

"Okay."

"Now take that box off so we can see what we are dealing with."

I reached for the blue box and took it off the test.

I didn't know whether to feel happy or sad. I felt numb within the three seconds it took me to register the big black word.

PREGNANT.

I was carrying my ex-boyfriend's brother's baby, who wanted to be fuck buddies with me.

When I thought about the situation, it was almost comical. Not in a funny way. More of a 'what the fuck?' kind of way.

"Holy shit." My best friend took the words right out of my mouth. "You're—"

"I'm pregnant."

Chicago was like the gift that just kept on giving.

NATE

"What has you all happy?" Xander grumbled beside me.

We had just clocked out of our 24-hour shift, and now it was time to head home. I, for one, was thrilled. I got to see Amelia.

I texted her throughout my shift, but she sounded slightly off. I had only received three memes within one shift. Usually, she sent me at least a dozen and then would make jokes when I told her I didn't get some of them.

I tried her phone a few times. She told me she was caught up with something and would call me back. That had been hours ago.

I know I sounded like a lovesick puppy.

"Earth to my best friend who refuses to give me the time of day." Xander waved his hand in front of my face. "Did you even hear what I said?"

"You asked why I'm so happy."

He frowned. "I did. But I also said something after."

"Oh, I wasn't paying attention."

"Of course, you weren't," he grumbled like a baby. "I was asking if you know if Amelia had spoken to Selena."

I shook my head. "I don't know. Why do you want to know about Selena? Don't you have her number?"

He scratched the back of his head, his face taking on a very light pink tint.

My face pulled into a shit-eating grin. "Don't tell me she's ghosting you."

He pushed my shoulder, almost making me fall into my locker. "Do I look like the kind of man who would get ghosted?"

He had gotten ghosted. What was even funnier was his sheer denial of it. Never had I seen this man sweat over a woman, yet here was this 5'6" woman making him stressed.

The man moved through women faster than he moved through underwear.

"Stop smiling, dammit." He slammed his locker shut and hooked his bag over his shoulder.

I threw my head back and laughed. I closed my locker and followed behind him while he sulked in silence.

"I just don't get it."

The poor guy looked lovesick. "One moment, I was ramming her on the kitchen counter, and the next, she cut me off like it meant nothing—oh my God, I sound like a chick. What the hell is wrong with me?"

We broke through the door and waved goodbye to our colleagues as they took over the next shift for us.

"Easy, you're whipped. Utterly and stupidly whipped." I patted his back. "There is no shame in it. I think that I—"

All the joy wholly drained from my system when I saw a familiar figure standing by my truck with his hands in his pockets and cigarette to his lips.

"Wait, is that…" Xander's voice trailed off.

"My little brother."

What was he doing here in Illinois?

Jacob lifted his head and saw me.

It was like I was looking at the younger version of my father. He was our old man every bit, just like I was every bit our mother.

He lifted his hand before throwing away his cigarette and approaching us. I had no idea why he was up here, but for some reason, I suspected that it had to do with the woman who had found a home in my heart.

"What are you doing here, Jake?" That was the first thing I said to him.

This was the first time I was seeing my brother in the flesh for maybe five or six years, and that was the first thing I said to him.

"No, 'hey brother, I missed you'?" he joked, but he sighed when he saw I wasn't smiling. "That's one of the reasons that I came to see you."

"And the other?"

"What?"

"You said, 'one of the reasons,' so what is the other reason you are here?"

"I came for Amelia."

My blood ran cold. Every last cell in my body turned frosty and rigid.

"I made a mistake."

And just like that, my brother snubbed every ounce of happiness I had acquired within the last few months.

You have got to be fucking kidding me.

29

NATHANIEL

The drive back to my apartment was silent. I was still trying to process that my little brother was in Chicago, and he was here to take the woman I was falling in love with away from me.

Once again, all things Braven Bay were being taken from me.

Why couldn't he stay on his side of the state line? Illinois, especially Chicago, was mine. Yet he had come to taint it for me too.

"Are you going to tell me why you're acting like I killed your cat?"

My hand tightened around the steering wheel. "What are you talking about, Jacob?"

"You're mad, and I don't know why. Is it because I came unannounced? You're the one that refused to come to Braven. You should have guessed I would eventually make my way down here."

"I would rather you didn't." I was being snippy with him. And from his perspective, it was uncalled for. But from my perspective, he was here to steal my girl.

But was she my girl? I had no actual claim to her. But that didn't make my feelings for her any less valid.

"What's your issue with me?"

I pulled into the downstairs parking and cut the engine off once I got into my spot. I didn't bother to wait for him. I just grabbed my bag and left. I headed for the elevator, hoping he would get the hint and not follow me. But I heard his footsteps.

We got in and a loud silence blanketed us. The tension was so thick it was suffocating. I didn't want to be in here with him, and I sure didn't want him to see Amelia. At least not until I spoke to her first. They had a past that I knew I couldn't compete with. And our history was… complicated at best. I held this long grudge against her, and now…well, I loved her. With every last ounce of my being, I loved that woman and wanted her to choose me.

But how could I compete with almost a decade of loving someone?

The door opened, and I made my way to my apartment. Thankfully I was on the other side of the floor. I didn't want him running into her.

I opened the door and he followed inside.

"I could have dropped you off at your hotel." I put my bag on the couch and turned to face him.

"I need to talk to you." He went to sit on the couch. "Please."

I walked over to the armchair to the side and sat down. I leaned back into the cool material and waited for him to start.

"I fucked up." He placed his arms on his knees. "I need her back."

"Amelia?"

He lifted his head. "Who else would I be talking about?"

"Why the sudden change of heart?"

"She's the one." He reached inside his back pocket and took out a small box. He opened it, and my blood stilled.

"Mom's ring." My voice was locked in my throat. "Dad gave it to you?"

"Yes." There was a slight smile on his face. "Do you think she will like it?"

I bit down on my tongue. The bitter taste pulled into my mouth, further souring my mood.

He wanted to marry her.

"I don't think you should ask her to marry you."

"Why?" His eyebrows pulled together. "I know I messed up, but we have been together for years, and there is love there. Hell, she moved to a different state to escape me. I know she still cares."

But did she?

I had wanted to ask her about it but had yet to get around to it.

The truth of the matter was that I was jealous. Jealous of his connection with her and jealous that he had a piece of her heart. I had yet to learn where I stood with her. Our agreement had been set, and we knew the terms and the conditions I had put in motion.

"I thought you said you needed more. Is she suddenly enough for you?"

His frown deepened. "What is up your ass? I was wrong before. Now I know what I want, and it's her."

"Are you sure?"

"What is your issue with me, Nathaniel?" he scowled. "I know her far better than you do."

"Do you?" I had never wanted to punch my brother more than I did then. "Do you even know where she is? Where she lives? How has she been doing?"

"I know she is in the city and will contact her. I just needed to get my shit together first."

"So you don't have a real plan. You're just going to show up at her doorstep with a ring in hand and a question you aren't even sure she will say yes to."

"She'll say yes."

"How do you know?" I fired back at him.

I was doing a piss poor job of hiding my irritation, but I was never good at faking things anyway. He was moving in on what was mine.

Why did he have to come now?

"She isn't some yo-yo that you can play with. You can't dump her and suddenly decide you want her again."

"That's why I'm here with this." He raised the ring in the air.

"And you think that will fix it all? Do you think you are magically putting it on her finger will make her want you again? What if she's moved on?"

"She wouldn't have. It hasn't even been a full year since the breakup. There is no way that she has forgotten about me."

"Hmm," was all I said to him.

The mother fucker was so overly confident that it annoyed me. Who was he to say that she hadn't moved on? He didn't have a permanent place in her heart. She wouldn't have allowed me to touch her if she hadn't moved on. She wouldn't have allowed me to make love to her the way I did the other day.

"Whatever." he got up from his seat. "I wanted to come here and see you, but as usual, you are acting like a complete and utter asshole. I won't bother sending you an invite to the damn wedding."

"There won't be a wedding." I should have kept my mouth shut, but he kept talking, which annoyed me now.

I watched his body go visibly tense. He took one long

look at me, and maybe it was the look on my face that said it all, but realization dawned on his features.

"You mother fucker!" The venom in his tone coated his words. "When?"

It didn't take a genius to know what he was asking about. But I kept my mouth shut.

His nostrils flared, and his fists balled at his side. "Where is she?"

"You don't need to know that." I slowly stood to my feet.

"How long have you been fucking her?' This time his voice raised an octave. "What? Cat got your tongue, brother?"

I looked him dead in the eye. "I think it's best you leave."

"I'm not going anywhere until you give me some answers."

We stared at each other, neither wanting to back down. My brother and I were never close, but we had never looked at each other with this much resentment and anger all because of the woman who had stolen our hearts.

"I don't owe you anything."

"The hell you don't!" He roared with the fury of a thousand lions. "You have been sleeping with my girlfriend behind my back."

"She isn't yours."

"Neither is she yours," he said. "How can she be after what happened all those years ago?"

My body went rigid. "That was in the past." I never told Jacob of the connection to Amelia and our family. My father must have told him.

"Really? Because last I heard, you hated her because you thought she killed Mom. So suddenly, that's changed? You finally forgave her for something she never did."

"That is none of your concern."

He paused for a second. I could see the wheels turning in his head. "You haven't told her."

I stayed quiet, which was enough of an answer for him.

He let out a humorless laugh, "You are one sick bastard. You want to be with her, yet you haven't told her about that night. The night that changed the entire trajectory of her life."

"I will...eventually."

I was going to tell her the truth of the matter that I was scared. I was scared I could lose her and wouldn't have her anymore.

"How can you hide that you were the car she and her mother crashed into that night? Does she know how much you wished her dead? The number of times you prayed that her life would be taken instead of mom's."

I remembered everything, and I resented myself for it. She never deserved that from me, and it took me falling in love with her to see that.

"I'm going to tell her." I didn't know if I was telling him or myself. For weeks I had been putting it off.

"Liar. You will continue to brush shit under the rug and will it all away the same way you handle everything else. You hide in this city away from Dad like he doesn't mean shit to you. Do you know how messed up that is?"

"Don't act like Dad didn't blame me for Mom's death."

His eyes narrowed. "He was grieving. He said things he didn't mean, and he said he was sorry. But you're the one who can't get over it enough to see that he loves you. Do you even know he's sick?"

My heart stopped. "What?"

"It's why he wanted you home for Thanksgiving. It's why he's been trying to get you home for the past three years. But you ran away to the military so you wouldn't have to deal with the pain. Or deal with your internal hatred."

I had enough. I didn't need to hear this, least of all from him.

"Get out."

He huffed, his eyes still locked on me. "Gladly."

He turned and stormed toward the door, ripping it open.

Shit.

Standing there on the other side of the door was Amelia. Her eyes were wide and red. She had heard us arguing on the other side, and she had been crying. Her eyes shifted from me to my brother and then back again.

"Amelia…" I moved toward her, but she shook her head, taking a few steps back.

It was clear in her eyes to see that she knew. The hurt in her eyes was my undoing. I couldn't help the pain that pooled into my chest seeing her look so…lost.

"I need some air." She turned and charged down the hall.

My brother chased after her, but I stood rooted in my spot, unable to move. I should have gone after her. I should have run after and gone on my knees begging her for forgiveness, but I did none of those things. I just stood there at a complete loss.

A foreign sting behind my eyes began to build, and my vision blurred ever so slightly. My chest squeezed, the pressure on my walls tightening.

I could feel myself collapsing and my life crumbling, but I could do nothing to stop it. All I could do was breathe through it and hoped that after all the walls had fallen, something would be left in the wreckage to salvage.

30

AMELIA

I could not believe what I had heard. My entire world tilted on its axis as all the dots started connecting.

I only had snippets from that night. Little scenes where I noticed a prominent figure that had pulled me out of the wreckage. For years I had fought with my memories to try to remember him. Now, low and behold, it was him.

The man who had saved me and given me a second chance at life. The same man that I had fallen in love with.

"Amelia…" his voice didn't even sound like his.

My eyes moved to meet his. For months I had stared into those mesmerizing orbs, entirely and utterly encapsulated with their beauty. But here I stood, looking into the eyes of a stranger.

I shook my head, not fully believing what I had just heard. "I need some air."

I turned and bolted down the hallways toward the staircase. I heard my name being called, but I didn't stop to figure out which brother it was.

He had been in the other car.

That night, it connected us—this tragedy where we had lost the most important people in our lives.

His coldness and resentment all made sense now. It was why had he done all he could to not be around me when I was dating his brother. I was a reminder of the night he had lost it all. I had survived, and his mother had not.

Someone called after me again, but I didn't dare to look back. I just kept running until I made it to the stairs. I had only broken out onto the foyer when a hand came over my wrist.

"Lia, wait."

I tried to pull my hand out of Jacob's grasp, but it was like iron. There was no way he was letting me go. I whirled around and glared at him.

"Please just leave me, Jacob. I don't want to talk right now." I ripped my wrist out of his hold.

This was the first time I was seeing him in months. I had expected to feel that familiar pang of hurt that had been evident when I first got here, but there was nothing. I felt nothing at all.

All this time, he had known about the accident. I had cried in his arms as I tried to remember that night. I only had little snippets of that night, and when I finally woke up from my coma, I was told my mother had died.

Had he known the truth?

"Why?" My voice sounded so cold and distant. I didn't even recognize it.

"Amelia, I…" he couldn't even continue.

"For years, I cried to you about that night. I told you about the man who had pulled me from the fire. I felt I owed my life to the man who had saved me. And you knew all this time. You knew, and you said nothing."

My voice raised, and people began to look our way, but I didn't care what people thought.

I wasn't mad that he had been there but was upset that they hid it from me. I deserved to know.

"I didn't know. I promise. Not until recently. My father knew, and he told me recently. But if I did, what good would it have done? Would it have brought your mother back?"

"I still deserved to know. I was in that accident, not you."

"And my mother died in it too!" He boomed back.

"And so did mine!"

Pain. That was the only thing that I could feel right now. But it was that emotional pain that was now manifesting into the physical.

My chest squeezed tightly, the walls of my heart constricting. I clutched my chest, willing my lungs to continue to breathe. The room tilted, and my balance faltered for a second. Thankfully, Jacob was there to help steady me.

"Amelia?" His voice sounded so distant like I was under-water. "Amelia?"

My body lost all its strength, and I tumbled to the floor. But just before my head could hit the ground, I was caught. My eyes stared up at the ceiling, the blood rushing past my ears and obscuring my hearing.

I blinked, trying to focus on my blurring vision.

"Someone call…" I couldn't catch the last bit of his sentence.

Jacob came into view, his panicked face filling my vision. "Stay awake for me, okay? Someone, please help!"

I turned my head slightly toward him. "The baby…"

That was the very last thing I remembered before my eyes closed on me. I tried to fight against them, but I had no strength. My body didn't feel like my own.

The last thing that weighed heavy on my chest was that I would never get to tell the man that I loved and that he owned my heart.

How much time had I wasted being scared? How much time had he wasted not telling me?

That was the problem with us humans: we put off things until it was the very last second—until it was all too late.

AMELIA

"It's coming down tonight," my mother stopped at the traffic light. She then turned to me with a slight smile on her face. "Why the long face?"

"I don't want to go to a new school."

We had just moved to Braven Bay a week ago, and I struggled to say the least. I wouldn't say I liked change, it was the hardest thing for me, but Mom wanted me to embrace the adventure.

I saw no adventure in this place. It was a small town with people so tightly knit together that they had already formed friend groups. I was the new girl—the alien.

I hated standing out; nothing stood out more than being the new girl.

"Bubs," she said, reaching over the console. "Moving here is a big adjustment; I promise you will love it."

Braven Bay, Wisconsin- This was my mother's old hometown, at least from birth to age 14. We were here and I didn't know how to feel. She was happy, but I was lost.

I was happy back home. I had friends. I had a life. And here I knew no one.

"Okay, how about this? Just give me one year, and if you don't like it, we'll move back to Minnesota."

My ears perked up. "Really? You aren't just pretending?"

"Now, why would your mother fib to you?" The light turned green, and she drove forward. "A deal is a deal. But I think I will win; Braven Bay has a way of growing on you."

I highly doubted that, but I didn't correct her. "You have a deal, Mommy."

She extended one of her hands toward me, "Shake on it?"

I approached the console to shake her hand, but everything flipped.

One moment we were driving calmly, and then the car swerved left. My mother cursed under her breath and tried to correct it, but it was too late.

The scene moved in slow motion. I watched it all play out like a terrible movie.

Headlights from the other side of the road flashed, and loud honking sounds could be heard before the unmistakable sound of metal smashing against metal and glass shattering.

I turned to my mother, who looked at me with horror painted on her features. She removed her hand from the steering wheel and clutched my hand in hers tightly.

"Close your eyes," I heard her scream.

I did as I was told, my brain still not fully registering what was happening.

After I closed my eyes, I don't remember what happened. I knew the car flipped at least twice. But during the initial impact, it was all somewhat of a blur.

My seatbelt kept me bonded to my seat, and my mother's hand never once left mine.

When I opened my eyes again, I wasn't in the car. Instead, I stood a few feet away, looking at the wreckage. I saw my mother's Toyota mangled and destroyed. The windshield completely shattered, and blood spattered on the front. The rain continued to pour down, and the thunder roared, shaking the atmosphere.

To my left was the blue jeep that had hit us or whom we had rammed into. I could see a woman lying on the hood of the car, entirely still.

Mrs. Cane.

I was watching the accident.

I wanted to rush over to her, but my feet stayed rooted. My eyes set on the woman I had never met but had heard so much about. The blood and the rain darkened her blonde hair. Her face was turned away so that I couldn't see her face.

"Mom," the broken voice of a boy whose heart was breaking filled my ears. "Mom?"

That's when I saw him.

"Nathaniel." I tried to speak against the lump that had formed in my throat.

I watched him amble out of the car, his face and hands cut and bleeding, the side of his head also oozing blood. His face was the same but just younger.

"Mom!" He screamed, limping toward his mother. I could feel the brokenness in his tone, the helplessness that weighed on him. "Please, God. No, no, Mom, wake up! Wake up!" His screams were like razor blades to my chest. Sharp piercing sounds that clawed at my eardrums.

I wanted to move and help him but I was rooted in my place.

My gaze shifted back to our car. I could see my mother staring over at my body. My chest rose and fell slowly as I struggled to breathe. I could see the glass surrounding me and the sharp cuts it had made on my soft skin. My mother's mouth pooled with blood, her eyes depicting the one emotion I didn't want to see in them—fear.

A slight sparking sound filled the air just after the boom of thunder. This caught Nate's attention. He looked at the car with

177

tears in his eyes. But then my mother turned her head and looked into the eyes of the poor teen who clung to his dying mother.

A silent conversation passed between them. I didn't know what was said, but somehow he understood what she wanted because he limped to the car toward the passenger side the next moment.

He tried to open the door, but it was initially useless.

"Save...her....:" my mother choked out. Or at least that was what I thought she said. It was hard to hear her above the thunder roar and the heavy rain pounding.

Nate pulled harder on the door until it finally opened. My body was still stone, and my hand was safely clutched in my mother's.

I wanted to move closer to hear what they were saying, but I was still held captive in my place.

She choked a few words, which Nate nodded to before he took me into his arms. He pulled me out of the car and hobbled his way away from the vehicle.

He had gone a few feet when a loud boom threw us to the ground as the car caught fire. Nate used his arms to break my fall and covered me with his body. He let out a low hiss, his skin brushing against the tar of the road.

I looked up to see the car I had been in only seconds prior come ablaze with my mother still in it. The flames proliferated, effectively engulfing her. I had expected to hear screaming, but there was nothing that came.

Had she died before the flames had consumed her? Was her body not in any pain?

Was this what had happened?

All these questions circled my mind, but I knew that no one could give me the answers.

I had imagined she had died on impact and felt no pain,

but this....knowing that there was a possibility that she had suffered so terribly shattered me.

I heard a little groan and looked at where Nate and I were. My little body squirmed under him, a soft and low whimper coming from my lips.

"You're okay," he whispered.

The sound of sirens filled the air. The red and white flashes come in the far distance.

Nate's body relaxed a little, his attention moving back to me. "You're okay. Help is coming."

He then looked over his shoulder to where his mother lay. "Hold on, Mom. Hold on."

It was the desperate prayer of a terrified son. I could feel the pain and fear that had engulfed him.

The scene before me began to fade away slowly. The pieces of the accidents disappeared until the only thing left was me in the darkness.

Watching it all play out this way made every sealed wound reopen.

My knees slowly gave out, and my body tumbled to the floor. I braced myself with my hands as I tried to control my breathing.

He had carried this weight with him all this time like I had taken my grief. Our scars were similar in shape, but the blade that had made each one differed.

"Oh, Nate." My heart bled for him, and my soul mourned for the boy that died that day.

I watched the light dimming from his eyes as tears streamed down his face.

The world had been cruel to him and marked him with a dark cloud. And it pained me that I was a stark reminder of all that he had lost that day—all that we had lost.

3 2

NATHANIEL

The gentle beating of the machine filled the room. My hand was clutched in hers tightly, hoping to feel a twitch or any pressure.

She had been like this for hours, and the doctor had said there was nothing to worry about, but how could I not worry?

A baby.

My throat tightened at the thought of our little one growing inside her. The times she had been sick and weak. She hadn't been fighting off some virus; she had been with child—our child.

I brought her hand to my lips, kissing it back and closing my eyes.

I was not a religious man, not by a long shot. I had given up on God when he took my mother from me. But here I was, begging for Him to spare the life of the woman I loved.

"Wake up, Amelia," I whispered into the silent room. "Please."

She was hooked up to an IV, and her vitals were good. The doctor had told me not to worry, but how could I not?

The last time I had been in a hospital, it had been with her in similar circumstances. Her on the bed and me in the chair looking at her. But unlike before, I wasn't asking for a trade. I was begging for mercy.

The door to her room opened, and in walked Xander and Selena. They had been here with me since yesterday and had done their best to keep my calm, but I was on the brink.

The longer she stayed like this, the higher my anxiety rose.

I cared for a few things, but she was at the top of my list. She was my world—my universe. Life didn't make sense without her, and I couldn't lose her, unlike how I had lost my mother.

"How is she?" Selena came to the other side of the bed and looked down at her best friend. "There's more color in her face."

She was lying. Amelia looked as pale as a ghost. But I knew she was only saying it to help me heal. But I didn't want false assurances. I just needed her to wake up.

That was it.

"Have you eaten?" Xander came up behind me and placed a wrapped sandwich in front of me. "You won't be useful to her if you are weak."

I shook my head. "I'm not hungry."

"You need to eat," Xander tried to push me. "Or let's at least get some air. You've been in here for hours."

I shrugged his hand off my shoulders. "I'm fine."

"Xander's right, Nate. You need to take care of yourself to take care of Amelia."

"Fuck off," I snapped.

Selena glared at me before she said, "I know you're a little stressed right now, but you don't have to be a raging asshole. I'm only trying to help."

"Help?" I scoffed. "You didn't tell me she was pregnant."

"Because she didn't want me to. Forgive me for honoring my friend's wishes."

Both of us were on edge. One of the people we loved most was unresponsive in a hospital bed. It was all a waiting game at this point, and with each hour ticked by, my optimism faded.

"If you had told me—"

"Then what, Nathaniel?" she fired back. "Could you have stopped this? You're the bloody cause of this whole thing. How can you not see that? She's pregnant because of you. She was stressed because of you, and now she finds out you were there when her whole world fell apart, and you lied about it. And instead of being nice to her all these years, you took out all your guilt and self-resentment on her knowing damn well she never deserved that!"

"Selena," Xander tried it interject.

"No, Xander. Someone needs to tell him like it is. What do you think will happen when she wakes up? Do you think that she will welcome you with open arms? Do you think she will forget that you hid this from her? That you played pretend for years? Do you know the toll her mother's death had on her?"

The silence that passed between us was thick. Not one word was uttered as her words sunk deep into my skin.

She was right.

Every last word she had spoken was nothing but the truth. Amelia was here because of me.

"You have the fucking audacity to tell me to fuck off when you are the main contributor to her pain and turmoil."

"Selena, enough!" Xander bellowed.

"Don't." I looked down at the woman I loved. She looked so peaceful like she was sleeping. Images of that little girl I had saved from the wreckage filled my mind. Her soft whimpers and tear-stained eyes had searched for her mother as I covered the destruction behind me. "She's right."

"Nate…"

I shook my head. "I think it's time I get that air after all."

I leaned forward and kissed Lia's cheek. When I pulled back, this heavy weight came to rest right in the middle of my chest. I turned to my best friend, gave him a curt nod, and walked to the door.

I was almost out when I heard their voices.

"Selena?" Xander hissed.

"What?" Selena snapped back.

I shut the door behind me and walked down the hallway with no real destination. All I knew was that I needed to reset and refresh my mind. Selena's words repeatedly played in my mind like a broken record.

I picked up the pace until I finally came to the door that led to the terrace. Once I broke through the threshold, I felt the cool air hit my face. I walked over to the terrace ledge and held my head to the night sky.

The moon hung high in the sky without a single star in sight. The busy Chicago streets echoed up here on the fourteenth floor of the building.

How had I allowed it all to go so wrong? I was meant to stay away from her. To give her the space to live her life away from my darkness. But somehow, life had brought us back together again.

I had fought her. I had fought us. And just when I was ready to accept what our future could hold, I destroyed her. I went back on the promise that I had made to her mother.

"You look like shit," a familiar voice said from the other end of the long terrace. I looked to my left and found my brother smoking something. "Before you go all dad on me, it's a CBD pen for my anxiety. I'm not an actual smoker."

"You're still here?"

He shrugged. "I'm not a complete asshole—contrary to what you think."

He took one more hit of his pen before he pocketed it in his jeans. He looked up at the sky, his body far more relaxed than mine. His head then turned to me, his eyes meeting mine.

Not a single word was spoken between us, but I understood what he was saying, and he understood me from the looks of it.

Truce.

We were waving the white flags and lowering our weapons.

33

NATHANIEL

A thick silence passed between us. Neither one of us wanted to say anything but needed to say what was weighing on us.

"There was a time I genuinely hated you." My brother was the first to pierce through the silence. "It was when you decided to leave for the military only a few years after Mom died. You left me and Dad alone to deal with the grief and the pain while you ran away. We had to sit in the pool of despair and wade through the rough waters."

I listened to the words I had been terrified to hear for years.

"Dad knew he messed up. He said things no father should and beat himself up for years trying to right his wrong. But how could he do that when his son wanted nothing to do with him?"

My father's words had cut far more than I allowed anyone to see. I was wrecked and still recovering from it all, and his cursing me out and blaming me for the crash was a stab to the heart. The words were a constant reminder in my mind.

I gulped, trying to fight back the sting that was assaulting the back of my eyes.

"He chased after you for years and years, and then he found out he was sick, and he fought in the hopes that maybe you would come back, so he held on—for you. I watched that man get on his knees and pray to a God he had stopped believing in to watch over and protect him while you were on tour. Do you know how hard it was to learn about your life through the social media of your buddies?"

I winced, realizing now just how messed up it had all been.

"When you got hurt, we thought you would come home, but you didn't. You only came after you had healed. Even then, you only stayed for three days before you left again to come here. You weren't a part of our family anymore, and I learned not to care anymore. But Dad never stopped. He held out the hope that one day you would change your heart."

He never gave up on me even though I had given up on him.

"Every time I called, you would be short with me and not want to talk. Whenever I needed you, you weren't there like you promised. I understand you were dealing with your shit, but I needed you, Nate. When Dad was depressed and popping pills like candy, I was scared out of my mind that I was going to lose him. But then I met Amelia."

At the mention of her name, my entire body ceased.

"She was like this ray of light that killed the darkness. She was my lantern, and I clung to her for dear life because she was the only thing that didn't feel…heavy." He let out a low and humorless laugh. "Of course, that was until I let her go, and it fucked everything up. But I couldn't lose her. She was the one good thing in my life and the only constant thing I had."

I knew that feeling well. That was precisely what she had been to me. She was like that for many people—this beacon of hope and light.

"So why let her go?" The words escaped my lips before I could even stop them.

He stared out at the skyline. "I had told myself it was because I needed more, but now when I look at it, I realize that I knew I couldn't keep her deep down. She had dreams far bigger than what I could give her. And I knew that with me, she was settling."

"So why—"

"—chase her down to Chicago and try to present her with our mother's ring?"

I nodded.

"Because I was scared." This was the most vulnerable I had ever seen my brother. He was not the kind of man who liked to show his scars. But here he was, bearing it all out for me. "I thought I could fight my darkness and become my own lantern. But the silence grew louder and the darkness thicker until I couldn't take it. Dad suggested therapy a few months ago. That's when I was diagnosed with moderate PTSD and moderate to severe anxiety. I got the pen to help me when I feel the symptoms creeping up on me."

"Amelia being away from you brought back the memories of Mom?" Was that why he had been hitting the pen?

He nodded. "She's my main trigger—mom, that is. And somehow, I had made Amelia the antidote to that trigger. I knew it was unfair to her to have her carry that kind of responsibility, especially because she didn't even know she was taking it.

We fought more and more when I felt she wasn't doing her 'job' of removing the darkness. But instead of blaming me, I placed it on her and came up with a bullshit excuse."

I had no idea this was the pain he had been carrying

around. But how could I? I ran from him. I declined invitation after invitation.

"I realize now that although I love her, I can't keep using her as my crutch." He turned to me fully with a sad smile on my face. "It was never her job in the beginning to fix me. I had searched for someone to fill the void Mom left, but now I realize I have to fill that space with my love for myself. She deserves someone who can love her wholly and fully."

She did. She deserved the kind of love that was soft and felt like warmth.

"She deserves you," my brother finished, completely stunning me into silence.

"She deserves more than me."

"Are you in love with her?"

"Of course I love her." My answer was immediate and without hesitation.

"But that wasn't my question, though, brother. I asked if you were in love with her. There is a difference between the two. One is where you are deeply rooted and embedded in someone else's soul. Their very essence and presence are both your destruction and salvation. There is no part of you that person has not touched."

Soulmates.

That's what he was trying to explain to me.

"Do you feel that way about her? Do you feel like she has embedded yourself and you in her?"

I nodded.

"Then I don't see why you're not the one she needs." He dug into his pocket and pulled out the small velvet box that housed our mother's ring. "This is rightfully yours, and it should be on her finger."

I stared at the box in complete and utter shock. Slowly, I took it out of my brother's hand.

"And I hear I'm going to be an uncle," he sighed,

returning to the view before us. "Hopefully, you don't keep the baby away from Dad and me too."

I swallowed hard, trying to dislodge the blockage in my throat. "I fucked up, Jake. I let my insecurities filter into my relationship with you, and I am so sorry. I was dealing with the guilt of losing Mom and trying to remove all negative emotions. I should have done better. I should have been better."

"You know that accident was no one's fault. It was an awful day and everyone got caught in that storm. It was an accident. ACCIDENT." He draped his arm over my shoulder. "Forgive yourself for being unable to play God and save our mother's life. And give yourself grace, Nathaniel. You saved the woman you loved and must stop living in the past."

"I don't even know if she will forgive me." I choked on my words, the possibility of losing her ripping at my insides. "And now with the baby...."

"This is Lia we are talking about. The woman leads with her heart and would never hold that night against you. If she needs time, give her time, but don't give up on her. I have never seen your eyes so alive since Mom died. It's like you're a whole new man. She brings life out of you."

That was true. She did bring life out of me. She brought out the very best in me. I had never felt more at peace than when I was with her.

"I love her." Saying those words out loud to someone other than myself was like breaking through the water and taking my first breath of air. "I love her, man."

"I know." He pulled me in for a hug. "I know."

This was the first time I didn't know how long we hugged like brothers. When we pulled apart, I knew this was the start of something new for the both of us. All that baggage and weight we had carried with us was falling off and we were on a new path—a better path.

My phone buzzed in my pocket, and my heart jumped when I pulled it out.

"She's awake," I whispered.

"That's great." He smiled, but as soon as he saw the look of terror on my face, he immediately shifted his stance. "It's going to be okay. Just breathe and listen to her."

I nodded.

"Let's go see your girl."

I hoped that she was still mine after we had our talk. But no matter what, I was not giving up on her or us.

34

AMELIA

Whan I woke up I was confused, but it all came flooding back. I first clutched my stomach and looked at my best friend, who reassured me that the baby was fine and was in no danger.

When the anxiety subsided, I began to wonder about the father of my child. I had expected him to be here but only saw Selena in the room.

"Where is he?"

"He went out for some air," she frowned a little, holding tightly onto my hand. "I told Xander to go and get him when you woke up."

There was something in her tone that didn't sound right.

"What's wrong?"

"What do you mean?" I could tell by the way she wasn't holding eye contact that she was hiding something from me, but I didn't know what.

"You have this face."

"I don't have a face."

"Yes, you do," I said, gesturing to her. "Whatever it is, you can tell me."

"I don't want you to get mad at me."

"Why would I get mad?"

She moved her gaze to meet mine, and I saw the guilt swimming in them. "I may have said something to Nate."

"What?"

And then she told me.

I was not surprised at all that she reacted that way. Selena had always been protective over me. Since we became friends in elementary school, she always tried to keep me safe from any danger—even at times from myself.

"I know you care about him, but I just…" she licked her lips, placing her hand on mine. "I can't watch you wither the way you did with his brother. These Cane men have taken so much from you. They have tampered with your heart, and you…you don't deserve that."

I placed my other hand on top of hers. "I love you for wanting to care for me and put me first. But it would be best if you let me make these choices for myself. I know you don't want to see me in pain, but the pain is inevitable. It's something that is almost a guarantee.Choosing to love this man could bring so much pain because Nathaniel Cane is not someone you can get over. He could be my ruin. But he could also be the most beautiful thing in my life—and I'm willing to take the risk. I'm ready to allow myself to free fall and chance not being caught by him because not trying at all could be the biggest regret of my life."

She nodded in understanding, but I could still tell from her face that she still had reservations. "I will be watching him closely, however. You know you're my girl and will always come first."

"I know." I pulled her down toward me so I could hug her. "You're the best."

She tightened her hold on me. "Bitch, I know. I'm literally like the start of your universe."

We chuckled, pulling away from each other.

The door creaked open, and Xander walked in with Nate behind him.

As soon as my eyes locked on him, everything else faded.

"We will give you two a moment," Selena said.

I barely even registered our two friends leaving the room.

When the door shut behind them, he and I were alone.

I stretched out my hand toward him. "Come here."

His legs moved, but his face remained passive. It was almost like he was trying to gauge just how I would feel. When he got to the side of my bed, his hand came in mine, and I let go of the breath I had been holding. His fingers interlaced with mine, and our gazes moved to where we connected.

Neither spoke, but a million different things were being said then.

I looked up at his face, and I could see the tortured look on his face. His eyes refused to meet mine, but his hold on me stayed the same.

"Nate," I called his name softly, but he didn't meet my gaze. "Look at me."

He stayed glued to our hands.

"Nate."

Nothing.

"Nathaniel, look at me."

He looked up finally, and I could see exactly what he felt. He opened his lips to speak, but no words came out.

"I love you," were the three words I had been scared to tell him, but they felt right to say now. "I don't know when, and I don't know how I came to love you, but I just did. Your love crept up on me silently. It didn't announce itself loudly nor make a show of it like I'm used to. It came in softly and touched my heart gently, almost like a whisper."

His eyes shined down on me, giving me the encouragement I needed to continue what I was saying.

"I am so sorry you had to hold this darkness all on your own, your mother, my mother, and Andre. You had a mountain of pain to hold in such small hands, and I'm sorry we weren't there to help you with your darkness."

"Amelia, you don't—"

"Let me say this." I reached up to cup his cheek. "I love you, Nathaniel Cane, and nothing you say or do will change my mind. Should you have told me? Yes. But I understand why you didn't."

"You do?"

"I can't begin to imagine the pain you must have felt from that night. You were the only one who remembered it fully. But a part of you also died that night along with our mother. Your innocence was stolen."

My words filled the room, blanketing over us.

"I don't want you to think I'm not in this with you because I am. What happened that night was a tragedy and changed our lives for eternity. But it does not define us. You are a brave and strong human and are the sole reason I'm still alive today."

The tears pricked my eyes as my heart poured out all the emotion it had stored for weeks.

"I'm sorry." His voice was much huskier now, thick with emotion. "I'm sorry I didn't tell you. I thought I was doing the right thing by keeping it to myself. But after I told my father, I should have just told you. At the time, my excuse was that I didn't want to hurt you. I didn't want you to relive that painful night. I didn't want to give you new painful memories to store away."

"I know what happened that night." That dream had been so vivid. "At first, I didn't, but I guess I just…I saw it in my head when I passed out. I saw what you had to go through that night, and I know it couldn't have been easy."

He looked astonished. "What did you see?"

And so I told him. I told him about my dream from beginning to end. And the more I described, the more pain and sadness riddled his face.

"I never wanted you to know." He looked down at my hands. "I didn't want you to feel that pain of losing your mother. I didn't want you seeing her that way."

The lump came back again, lodging itself in my throat. "I know. But I needed to."

He used his thumb to wipe away the tears that had escaped from my eyes.

"I just want to know one thing."

"What?" He leaned forward, placing a kiss on my forehead.

"What did she tell you when she told you to pull me out? What did she whisper to you?"

The sides of his lips tilted upward slightly into a small smile. "She told me to take care of her special little girl and to keep her safe."

My heart faltered in my chest.

Oh, Mom. He did more than just that. He set me alight in ways that I had never imagined. He taught me what love could be and what it truly felt like. The kind of emotion that filled your entire body and tethered itself to your soul. It was like electric.

Before I knew it, we both had tears free-falling from our eyes. It was a mixture of both joy and grief.

Nate sat beside me, his entire posture changing as he held both my hands, crying.

"I'm not perfect, not by a long shot, but I will do my best to be a man deserving of you. I will make sure that every morning you wake up, I remind you just how beautiful you are. I will spend the rest of my days putting you first and ensuring you feel seen and heard."

"Nathaniel Cane, are you proposing to me right now?" My heart hammered in my chest. "Because if you are, I will have to stop you. I'm in a hospital gown and probably look like shit."

He chuckled, "Don't worry, I'm not proposing…yet. But what I am doing is trying to tell you that I love you."

I couldn't even contain the smile.

"I love you, Amelia. I think I loved you when I saw you walk out of our building looking sweaty and tired from moving all those boxes."

I shoved him away from me playfully. "Shut up."

"I want only you." His hand then moved to come and rest on my stomach. "I want us. I want the family life—the white picket fence and the kids running around making a mess. I want to create memories and a home with you."

"I want that with you too."

He leaned his forehead against mine and stared at me. "You and me against it all?"

I nodded. "Us against it all."

Our lips came together, almost like we were sealing the deal with a kiss.

I knew our journey was only beginning, and we had a mountain to climb when it came to what lay ahead, but I knew that if I had this man by my side, I could tackle it all.

He drew me into his chest and kissed my forehead when we pulled apart.

"By the way," I said into the thick of the silence, "before you even think of proposing, you will have to get on Selena's good side."

He groaned. "I thought as much. But even if she disapproves, who stops me from kidnapping you and taking you to Vegas for a little shotgun wedding action? I already knocked you up."

I rolled my eyes even though he couldn't see. "Leave it to you to skip a few important steps."

He pulled away, his face turning serious, "Okay then. I must make an honest woman out of you before our baby girl arrives...."

He hopped off the bed and got down on one knee.

"Don't you dare propose like this, or I swear you will regret it, Nathaniel. I'm in the wrong kind of gown," I pouted. "Propose to me when we are out of here. Not when I'm looking like I just fought through a war."

"You look beautiful."

"Don't lie."

"I'm serious. Baby girl has you glowing, baby."

I tilted my head to the side. "You think it's a girl?"

He nodded.

"I think it's a boy." I patted my still-flat belly. "But regardless of what it is, I just want him or her to be happy and feel all the love in the world when they arrive."

"They will," he returned to sit beside me, "I can't believe we made a baby."

"I can't believe I let you put a baby inside me."

He softly pressed his lips to mine, saying, "And I may just do it again a few more times after that."

"How many times are we talking here?"

"Well..."

Taking a chance and making a bold decision changed the course of my life. I don't know what would have happened if I had stayed in Braven Bay. But I took a risk, and it paid off. I am grateful for the new opportunities in my life, such as marrying my future husband and welcoming our beautiful baby boy or girl very soon. And quite possibly the white picket fence I had always pictured.

Did you like this book?
Then you'll LOVE Next Door Billionaire, Book 1 of the standalone series The Billionaires of Mystic.

Next Door Billionaire is AVAILABLE NOW ON AMAZON and Kindle Unlimited!
http://www.amazon.com/dp/B0C3JDTYQJ

Also! Follow me on Facebook for deals on new releases and weekly drawings!

https://www.facebook.com/Natalie-Belle-Contemporary-Romance-Author-106255492403271

DO YOU LIKE FREEBIE ROMANCE BOOKS?

Sign up for my newsletter and get Second Chance Billionaire for free!

One hot night with a Navy SEAL changed my life forever.

And now I see him reflected every day in the little girl he never knew we had.

My business is growing; except for the Billionaire Jerk standing in my way.

Now it's the fight of my life against the God Bod, real estate mogul.

There's one problem…. I never thought I'd see my one-night stand again. *Hotter and grumpier* than ever.
Sign Up Now!

https://dl.bookfunnel.com/wwy8q9smb3

Printed in Great Britain
by Amazon

37234760R00118